The Two Kingdoms

The Two Kingdoms

Kelsey Thomas

Printed in the United States of America

First Printing, 2021

ISBN 978-1-951883-47-8

Butterfly Typeface Publishing
PO Box 56193
Little Rock, AR 72215

This book is dedicated to my late father, William Thomas, my mother, Darlene Thomas, my family, and my friends. Thank you for all of your love and support!

"Imagine It. Believe it. Do it."

Table of Contents

Chapter 1

The Rumor

"Yawn," Wolverine said. "Another new day." I made up my bed and got dressed. I went to a building that had showers to wash. After I was done washing up, I took my laundry to the cleaners to make my clothes fresh. I only have three pairs of clothes for each day and they do need to hold on for a long while, so they are sturdy. The same goes for my two pairs of shoes that I travel in every day.

When I was done with everything, I waited for my best friends to come with breakfast. I sat at one of the tables outside the Barbecue Grill House. Ten minutes later I saw Madeline and Victoria rushing with our breakfasts in their arms. When they arrived to where I was, I asked, "Did you get me my favorite breakfast?"

"Yep, like always!" Victoria replied tiredly. As they settled down at the table, we dug in and ate. She was the first one to speak. "Man, I think the people who cooked this updated the taste. This is much better than before. How's yours, Wolverine?"

"Good, but mine tastes the same as always," I responded.

"Hmph," she added, "Guess I'm the lucky one."

"Victoria, you're always the lucky one!" Madeline laughed.

"Wonder why," Victoria said.

The conversation went on fine until Madeline explained to us about this rumor that had been spreading all over the world and it had been going on for so long. Nevertheless, it was remarkably interesting. It was so interesting that I decided to lean in real close. "Hey, you guys ever heard of this rumor that has been going on for so long?" She asked us.

"Which one?" Victoria asked back.

"The one about how there's only one person in the entire world that is actually the most powerful human in the world, of course!" Madeline said.

"Oh yeah, I've heard that," Victoria said.

"I haven't," I boasted out loud. They both looked stunned at me for a minute. "Is there something wrong?" I asked, puzzled.

"You've never heard?" They asked in unison.

"No," I repeated. "At least I don't think I have." They both looked at each other, then at me, then at each other again.

"OK," Madeline started, "the rumor is the most powerful rumor in all of humanity and someone in this world is the most powerful human in the world. They are supposed to be half angel and half demon. That person used to live in another world far, far away from here where demons and angels used to live. When the person is revealed and knows who they are, a light will appear from the sky that everyone in the world will see and take them to their old home."

"Oh, so—" She stopped me.

I'm not done yet, Wolverine, be patient," ordered Madeline.

"Sorry," I apologized.

"The reason for this," she started again, "is because thousands and thousands of years ago, demons and angels used to live happily because the person who lives in this world used to be in that magical world when they were just a baby. But that changed. Because of this, the demon lord of the demons did not approve of the baby and got angry. He got into an argument with the angels and the demons for several years, but no one knew why he didn't like the baby. Then, he had a plan. It was a good one too. He decided to sneak into the heavenly side of the kingdom and steal the baby to take it to another world, called Earth. The demon lord placed the child in an alley of this town. A day later, a couple who was already married saw the child crying and thought it was a great idea to take care of the baby. We don't know where that person is now, but all we know is that he or she is here in this world somewhere. That's it. The end."

"Wow," I said, "good thing you told me about it."

"No problem, it was my duty."

"Madeline, what was the demon lord's name?" I asked her.

"Ganon," she replied.

13

"Ganon," I repeated. "Sounds like that would be his name. Ganon."

After my friends and I finished eating, they told me their goodbyes and left. All that morning I thought about Ganon and all about what Madeline had said about the rumor. I could never get it off my mind. That's when I started to think about something else. I started to think that would help.

But when evening came, it came back into my brain again. I decided to eat something to clear it. There's this guy who works at this Chinese restaurant and he cooks me food every day. He sometimes teaches me new Chinese words to say. We're not typically best friends but instead, we're just friends. The best part is that he gives me free food! Which means I don't have to pay a penny. His name is Li Jun.

"你 好!" he said.

"你 好!" I greeted back.

"Guess what?"

"Another Chinese phrase?" I guessed.

"You got it. Listen close. Are you ready?"

"Ready when you are," I said.

"我 爱 你."

"我 爱 你." I repeated. "If 爱 means love, and 我 means I, then the sentence is maybe saying, I love you?"

"Yes, good job, Wolverine! In the next couple of years, you will be a natural at Chinese! Maybe you should say that to your friends and see their reactions sometime or other."

Oh, I will!" I said. As I picked up my food that I ordered, I started thinking about that rumor Madeline was explaining to me. I decided to tell him about it. "Li Jun?"

"Yes, Wolverine?"

"Madeline explained this old rumor to me about this angel and demon thing. Are you familiar with it at all?"

"Ah, yes, I've heard of that rumor before. Young people these days have been talking about it ever so long. I've wondered is it actually true," he said skeptically.

"You're probably right, but if the whole world is talking about it, then it has to be true," I reasoned.

"Maybe so," he said. We both paused for a second until I broke the silence.

"Alright, then I guess I will head back. Thank you for your opinion, Li Jun!"

"OK then, take care!" Li Jun waved.

As I walked along the sidewalks, I heard cultural music from outside a cultural shop. I mostly enjoy these sounds but Madeline and Victoria dislike them. Which isn't that shocking to me. When nightfall came, I started to stay up for a while by looking at all the stars and they were unbelievably beautiful indeed. There were thousands and thousands of them. I've always loved looking up at the stars. It makes me feel calm.

I got tired of looking at the stars, so I started telling myself goodnight. I kept thinking about that rumor again and it made me not want to go to sleep. But after a while I got sleepy after all and then before I knew it, I fell asleep. For a minute or two I slept soundly but then after that I saw something in my dream. It was a little scary.

The space that I was in was very dark and I really wanted to get out of there. It was also kind of cold in there too. After a while I saw two bright glowing eyes staring at me. One was white and the other, red. They both looked far away but somehow seemed close. The room was very silent and made me uncomfortable. So, I decided to say something. I didn't know what to say at first, which was hard for me. I decided to say this, "Who are you both?"

"We," said the angel, "are both messengers from each of our kingdoms. One of the guards from The Angelic Kingdom has sent us to Earth to give you this message."

"Why," I asked hesitantly. "Why are you telling me this?"

"Because," the demon began, "you are the chosen one, Wolverine, and you need to come back home," he said in a sad tone.

"What? I don't get it."

"You will eventually," he confessed.

"H-How will I?" I was so confused.

"Be patient, Wolverine, I know you want answers but just be patient. Patience will give you answers," said the angel.

"OK," I said.

"Look," the demon said, "ever since you've lived in this world, everyone from The Two Kingdoms has been watching you, even us. We have all even seen Madeline telling you about this world and we were pleased."

"And," the angel added, "the reason we are here is because Ganon is destroying our kingdoms. Since you are our only way of hope, The Two Kingdoms both agreed to find you because you were the one who kept our kingdoms from separating."

"Really?" I questioned the angel. I wondered could it be too good to be true.

"Yes," the demon responded. "You are our only way of hope because Ganon used to be our king, but he got worse in our kingdom and he tried to tear it apart. None of us demons knew why."

"And," the angel continued, "he's been ripping apart our kingdom as well and we angels never understood why either. Not even your parents."

"Parents?" I said, confused. "My parents are dead." I didn't know what the angel was talking about.

"Wolverine," the demon said softly, "do you remember the part Madeline told you about the baby being left in an alley?"

"Yes," I said. "What about it?"

"The baby was left in an alley and there was a couple who saw the baby and they decided to take care of it," the angel repeated.

"Yes, and?"

"They only found you, Wolverine," the demon said. "They are not your real parents."

"Then who are my real parents?" I asked them both.

"Your mother," the angel started while smiling, "is my queen."

"And your father," the demon started seriously, "is my new king."

"Wow," I said shaking my head in disbelief. "What are their names?"

"Your mother's name is Alice," said the angel.

"And your father's name is Amorok," said the demon.

"Alice and Amorok," I repeated.

"Yes," said the angel. "And our names are Ariella and Leroy."

"Wow," I said again. "So, what's next?"

"As morning comes, Wolverine, you will wait until your friends come and once they do, immediately tell them what we told you," Ariella instructed.

"But Ariella, what if they won't believe me?" I asked her.

"Don't worry because we've already taken care of that," she replied with a knowing smile.

"How is that?" I wondered.

"Leroy and I will give you some of our powers to you."

"OK," I agreed.

"But one more thing, before you wake up," she cautioned. "Once they believe you, we both will pick all three of you up and send you to The Two Kingdoms."

"Why, I mean, why do Madeline and Victoria have to come with me?"

"Your question won't be answered until we get there," Leroy said.

"Fine," I agreed. "So, what are my powers anyway?"

"Do not worry, Wolverine, you'll know when it's time. Goodbye, see you tomorrow," Ariella said, assuredly.

"Huh, wait, no! I have more questions!"

But after that, they were gone.

Chapter 2

I Am Ready!

I woke up breathing heavily and looked around. It was morning and everything was normal. It felt so real. I went to take a warm shower so I could relax. And it worked! But only a little. After I was done with everything, I sat at the table where my friends and I usually eat and waited for them to come so I could tell them what Ariella and Leroy told me. While I was waiting, I started to think that maybe what I saw in my dream was a joke and was not a real message, but I wanted to try it anyway. After about fifteen minutes, they arrived. "Victoria, Madeline! I need to tell you something!"

"What is it, Wolverine? Is there something wrong?" asked Victoria, worried.

"Not technically," I said. "It's something else."

"Phew," Madeline said relieved, "good thing. So, what do you want to tell us then?"

"It's about this dream I had last night and it's about what you were telling me about this angel and demon thing?"

"Yes, keep going," Madeline urged.

"This angel named Ariella and this demon named Leroy were telling me how I was the chosen one. Like, I was the baby that was in the alley and that they told me to tell this message to both of you," I explained.

"Why?" Victoria asked.

"I don't know," I told her. "She just said to tell you both." They stared at me for a while and then back at each other. Then, they started laughing. "What's so funny!" I asked.

"Wolverine, I think that dream you had last night is fake!" Madeline laughed.

"But—" I stopped.

Look," Victoria said, "whatever you just said didn't make no sense at all. Why would you think we would believe that?"

"B-But—"

"No, Wolverine, OK? You probably knew it was fake anyway, right?" Madeline questioned.

"Well," I started, "I didn't think it was fake because it looked like it was a message. Here, I'll prove it to you."

"But how?" Victoria asked.

"Ariella and Leroy gave some of their powers to me. They never showed me how to use them, but they just told me that I'd figure it out on my own," I explained.

"Um, OK?" Victoria said.

I got up and tried to show them my powers by closing my eyes and doing nothing. I knew that wouldn't work so I tried to do something else. I tried punching a mailbox with my fist and that didn't work either. But it was extremely painful though, ouch. I was almost about to give up until I had one more thing left to do. I raised up my right hand and then fire started blazing out from it. "Eeek!" I screeched. The flames rising from my hand terrified me. They were so huge! It didn't even hurt me though, which was surprising.

"Ah!" They both yelled.

"It's … real!" I said stunned.

"Do it again, Wolverine," Victoria shouted.

I lifted my right hand and the fire came back again. "Does it hurt?" Madeline asked.

"Nope," I replied. "Not a bit." As people walked by, I noticed that they were looking at me. Some of them looked and stopped to watch. Others were whispering to each other. The rest, well, they were looking but eventually got bored of watching and kept going. "Wow," I said amazed, "this is incredible." I've finally discovered one of my powers and I believe that is also one of Leroy's powers too. Then, something appeared in the sky. An opening had appeared, and the wind blew hard. Everyone in the town looked up to see what was happening. I too looked up as well as Victoria and Madeline. Just as Ariella and Leroy promised, they came to pick us all up.

"Who's that?" Madeline asked.

"Ariella and Leroy," I answered. As the opening in the sky closed, the two of them flew down toward us. Their wings looked so magical and so majestic. I was so thrilled; I didn't know what to do. "Ariella! Leroy! You're both actually here!" I said to them.

"Yep," Ariella said, "just like we promised."

"Woah," Madeline said as she took a step back.

"Madeline, it's OK. There's nothing to be afraid of," said Ariella.

"H-How do you know my name?" Madeline asked, trembling.

"Let's just say we know each and every person's name in this world," Leroy responded instead.

"OK," she said, still trembling.

"Madeline, for real, it's OK," I said.

"I know, but …" She paused.

"But she was so shocked that they're actually real," Victoria said, helping her finish her sentence.

"Yeah," Madeline said. "That's it."

"Well then, we need to head back. We cannot be late," said Ariella.

"Where are we going?" Victoria questioned.

"To The Two Kingdoms," I replied.

"The Two Kingdoms? What's that?"

"The Two Kingdoms is The Angelic Kingdom and The Demon Kingdom. That is where my real home is," I explained.

"Oh," Victoria said and gulped.

As Ariella and Leroy took us all three to The Two Kingdoms, I had a slight feeling that where I used to live was going to be beautiful and it was. When we got there, Madeline, Victoria, and I were in complete shock. It's like Kingdoms were separated as a community, but they were still whole as one kingdom. Angels and demons flew between the two different kingdoms greeting one another. It was just so magical.

When we got to our destination I looked all around, and it was pretty huge. I couldn't believe I actually came from such a place. It was so peaceful, compared to Earth. Ever since I'd been living on Earth, there was barely any peace. I've always hated society.

We walked to the Angelic side of The Two Kingdoms. Let me describe it to you. Everything was gold. The heavy golden double doors were so tall you couldn't even see the top. The pathway was made out of gold. The kingdom itself was shiny gold, and it looked like it could trick your mind into thinking it was touching the sky. The kingdom was ridiculously huge indeed and also incredibly beautiful. I wondered how these wonderful beasts made this tall structure.

Going inside one of the kingdoms was amazing. It felt like I was the main person to perform in an important event or something. What I saw in this area were rows and rows of angels and demons in facing me. A female angel and a male demon were facing me as well. "What's happening?" I asked Ariella nervously.

"Shh." She hushed me quietly. Then, we all stopped. I looked behind me and there was a demon guard with a spear that stared right back at me. I quickly turned around, thinking that wasn't a good idea and that I should probably not do that anymore. Then the angel who was in front of me spoke.

"Ladies and gentlemen, angels and demons, we are now going to welcome back Wolverine to The Two Kingdoms."

"Huh?" Madeline said. "If they're welcoming you, then why are Victoria and I here?"

"I don't know," I responded. "I am wondering the same thing." We all kept telling the angel about how grateful we were for arriving until she asked us did we have any questions. "I," I said immediately, "I have a question."

The angel looked and turned toward me and asked, "Yes, what is your question, Wolverine?"

I looked at her for a second and asked, "If you're celebrating and welcoming me back here to The Two Kingdoms, then why are my friends here?"

The angel nodded and replied, "Yes, that is a good question. After this speech, Amorok and I will tell you why."

"OK," I said. "Wait, I have one more question."

26

"I could be here all day," the angel said with a genuine smile.

"Are you my mom?" I asked quietly.

She smiled very brightly and nodded with a reply, "Yes, I am your mother and my name, as you may have realized, is Alice."

I grinned, knowing that I was right. Then as she started speaking again, I noticed the characteristics between the angels and the demons. When I dreamed seeing Ariella and Leroy, I noticed their facial expressions and their tone. As an angel, they sound so happy and bright but as a demon I could see their faces barely smiling and their voices sounded serious. They would barely smile. I guess that's just how they were, compared to angels. To be honest, I would rather smile all the time than to always have a dirty look on my face, every single day. It just looks better.

When the speech ended, Alice called Madeline, Victoria, and me to follow her and Amorok into another area. As we followed them, we went into a big room full of medieval books and scrolls. There was a long table made out of gold with golden chairs. I could see that Madeline was getting a little anxious and confused and I was kind of the same way. But it was a little cozy in there, so I tried to relax a little. At least that made me a little confident about what was going to be said.

"So," said Amorok, "the reason why all of you are in here with us is for two reasons. First, Wolverine, we wanted to give you an opportunity to say your last goodbyes to your friends here with us before they have to leave. Because, you have to stay here."

"Why do they have to leave?" I asked feeling sad.

"This is because of reason two, which I am going to talk about now. Wolverine, Alice and I and the rest of the angels and the demons have debated whether we should tell you to kill Ganon or not and most of them said yes."

"Me? But why me? I don't know how to fight and all of you know that."

Then Alice started to speak up. "Our people have tried to kill him but none of them succeeded. We both knew we had no other option, so we decided to ask our people if you could do it. Please understand that we had no other choice and, of course, we know that you can't fight but someone will teach you how. You just have to have faith. That's all it takes."

"Wolverine," said Amorok, "you *will* defeat Ganon once and for all. You may not believe it, but you have the strength, the speed, the skills, the power, and the courage. But do not worry, for you will not be alone because everyone will be inside your heart no matter what. You will journey to faraway lands and defeat monsters that Ganon has planned for you. Ganon already knew we had decided to send you off to defeat him with that stupid silvery-looking ball he always has when he tries to spy on people. Also, our people will provide you with everything you will need in order for you to go through your journey. If you defeat Ganon, you will be rewarded for life. Any questions before we leave?"

"First off, Amorok," Alice started to say, "there was no need for you to say the word *stupid*. We already knew it was an ignorant idea for that nosey one to spy on us, so you just could've skipped that useless word and just said something like, "With that silvery-looking ball he always has when he spies on people." That is a *much* better way to say that sentence. Also, it's not called a ball, it's called an orb."

I could hear and see the frustration in his eyes while he was mumbling when she was explaining that to him. As he rolled his eyes, he said, "Yes, dear, thank you for reminding me."

Madeline, Victoria, and I had gotten a little bit quieter than usual because the room paused for a moment. So, I decided to break the awkwardness by saying, "So, I have a question."

"Go ahead," he said, still frustrated at Alice.

"When will I be starting the journey?"

"In two days," he replied to me.

That made my eyes pop. "*Two days!?* That's not even enough!"

"I'm sorry but we had to," he apologized.

"I … I can't do this! I just can't! There has to be someone else who can do it because this all has to be a mistake!"

"Wolverine," Alice said a little stunned, "of course you can do it. It may not seem like you can simply make the journey that Amorok explained to you, but you can, and we all have faith in you. Even your friends."

I looked at Alice for a moment and then at my friends, then Amorok. "But what if—"

"There are no what ifs, Wolverine," Amorok stopped me, "you will be all right."

I huffed and looked down at the ground thinking, *Should I just accept my fate to help save my community? Should I just accept everybody's suggested compliments that I'll rise to the challenge?*

Then I got my answer.

"Well, are you going to kill Ganon?" Amorok asked.

"Yes," I responded.

Chapter 3

My New Friend

"Then for right now we will have to get you ready for it," Amorok said.

"What will I have to do?" I asked.

"Well," Alice remarked, "first you will have to do some basic training."

"Like, fighting?" I guessed.

"Yes," Alice replied. "But also skills to help you learn how to survive. Some of Ganon's traps are monsters that are incredibly powerful. That's why, here, we have trainers to help people like you to defeat Ganon. Many of our soldiers wanted to defeat him and so they went to battle. But they failed and a lot of them died a horrible death. This was largely because their skills were insufficient. But you, Wolverine, will have better training because we know that you are our only hope."

"OK," I said understanding this was my destiny.

As we were done with talking, Alice went to Ariella and Leroy to drop off my friends back to Earth. I knew I was going to miss them very, very much and they were going to miss me. During this journey, I had to remind myself that I would be fighting for them too. Then Alice told me to follow her into a room. She said I would have until one o'clock to get settled in, as it's around that time I would go into The Demon Kingdom.

"When you arrive at The Demon Kingdom, you will see me there," she said.

"Alright," I said.

At exactly one o'clock I immediately went to The Demon Kingdom to find Alice. When I got there, I saw Alice talking to a demon.

Is he my trainer? I wondered.

I walked toward them steadily, not wanting to interrupt their conversation. As I got closer, I stopped, thinking maybe I should just wait instead.

"No, no, no!" Alice said when she noticed me. "Come along, dear, no worries."

"Oh, OK then," I said, relieved. I walked toward the two of them so I could listen to what they had to say.

"Wolverine, this is Goliath, Goliath, this is Wolverine."

"Yes, of course," Goliath said.

His voice was very deep, and I noticed one of his eyes was green and the other, red. He had huge horns and he looked strong. He also had enormous wings with sharp tooth-like things at the end. And did I forget to mention that he looked like he was six feet, compared to my height of five foot six. So yeah, he was pretty tall.

"Wolverine," said Alice, "you do not have to worry because he will firstly show you the basics and then move up more levels. Remember, you only have two days before your journey, so try your best. Your training will only be for an hour. When you're done, Goliath will lead you back here. I will return here at two thirty to collect you."

"Yes ma'am," I said.

"You may now go," she said.

I went with Goliath through some hallways, up one flight of stairs, and into a room with the number 665 on the door. It was a big room with a lot of windows. Through the windows you could see a lot of structures and people from The Demon Kingdom and The Angelic Kingdom. You could even open the windows but not now. Maybe when I took a break I would, so I could have some fresh air.

After I was done exploring the whole room, I was ready to begin my first training at The Demon Kingdom. And, just as Alice said, it was a basic training, which consisted of surviving and fighting. After a lot of practice, we both took a break, and I experienced many things as well. To be honest, it was pretty fun. I enjoyed myself a lot. Goliath seemed like a nice guy, in spite of how he looked.

During the training, it was tiring and I probably lost a few pounds. It was a pretty big deal to do. "You did a good job back there with your fighting," Goliath said to me as we were going back to the main part of the kingdom to meet Alice.

"Thank you," I said, "I never knew I was ever actually good at stuff like this."

When we arrived to where Alice was, we said our goodbyes to Goliath, and then Alice and I left The Demon Kingdom. "How was it, Wolverine? How did you like your training? Do you think you did good? Was it alright?" asked Alice.

"Yes, yes, yes, and yes," I replied, annoyed.

"Good," she said relieved.

Later, the sky made its way into sunset and I was smoked. It was a long day indeed and my body began to shut down. The horizon was exceptionally beautiful, and it was satisfying to watch. Alice took me to The Angelic Kingdom inside a big bedroom with a nice big bed, which seemed to call for someone to lay down on it. The rest of the room contained a lot of interesting things.

"This bedroom will be permanently yours. Any questions before I leave?" Alice asked me.

"No, I'm fine," I told her.

She nodded as the door clicked shut. When she left, I surveyed the room a little bit more. There were some empty bottles on a counter. I noticed a little journal on a desk with a lamp and a glass jar full of calligraphy pens. Next to the desk was a medium-sized window with a vase of flowers. Then there was little nightstand on the right side of the bed.

And, of course, there was a closet for my clothes. Something caught my eye from underneath the bed.

I was just thinking about how maybe this room could be a mystery. Like maybe there could be a secret pathway to another dimension or to another room of some sort. Then I had an idea. I looked under my bed to see if there was anything. I got on my knees and crouched under. My body hesitated for a minute, I was hoping there wouldn't be any spiders or any insects crawling underneath. When I looked, I saw a little, golden, dusty chest box with a keyhole and a rusty golden key right beside it.

I pulled the little chest box and key toward me and shook it before opening it. It sounded like there was something solid in it. I stopped guessing and decided to open it up with the key and it came unlatched. As I opened it, I couldn't really see the odd figure because of the dust, so I blew on it. That's when I could see it properly.

It was a golden orb and with it was a written note. I couldn't read it well because it looked like it was written in some foreign language. I tried figuring out this weird language but then I gave up. I knew it had something to do with the orb surely. I played around with the figure for a while but then I got sleepy, so I went to bed right away.

The next morning, the sun was shining brightly. I opened up the window and felt a breeze blowing through my hair as I felt the heat's rays. The time I woke up was around nine o'clock. Before I was about to leave the room, I reached under the bed to grab the chest again and opened it.

I wanted to have contact with the orb a little bit more before I left.

The object didn't look like it could do very much. All I was able to do with it right now was hold it. That showed me it was just a regular golden orb. I placed the orb back inside the box, closed it up, and pushed it back underneath the bed. I started not to think about it too much. I was too tired to even try to figure it out.

I ran down the stairs and saw some people chattering and gathering outside. I went to see what was going on and that's when I saw it. It was a big, beautiful dragon and on top of it was a male angel, riding the beast. I didn't know what I was thinking, but I thought if I could have a pet dragon it would be awesome for my journey.

Thinking maybe I could see the dragon a little more, I squeezed through the crowd making my way toward the front. My eyes grew wide, amazed by the male angel sitting on the dragon's back. The dragon looked tamed and shy and he didn't seem like he was hurting anyone. He even seemed patient and kind. Did I forget to mention that he was extremely cute?

The dragon's skin color was black and purple, and his eyes were purple. He had a long, wavy tail with a triangular point at the end. His teeth and claws were very sharp and pointy. "Attention, everyone, attention," the angel started to say. "I know that all of you here are confused as to why this creature is here. So, I will explain to all of you why. This dragon that I have brought here was seen miles away from The Two Kingdoms. When I approached the animal, it seemed tamed and kind so I brought him here because he looked like he was lost, and I thought he would be safe here. But there's this one problem. Someone needs to take care of him."

"Me!" I blurted out. "I could take care of him." The whole crowd looked at me. Even the dragon.

"I'm sorry, Wolverine, but you don't look like you could take care of him, and besides you're just a kid and—"

"Silence," Alice said strictly.

"W-What?" he said.

"She can have him," she said.

"My queen, you don't understand. There's nothing your daughter can do with this beast. And, besides, she's just a child. What can she do with it?"

"She'll take him with her on her journey. On her journey she will not be alone for she will have to communicate with that animal and that animal will have to communicate with her. She will need him when battling and when in need of comfort and survival. That, Gabriel, is what she can do with it."

Gabriel and the crowd looked stunned and so did I because ever since I'd been here, I'd never heard Alice's voice like that. It was so demanding that it had caught me off guard. I looked at Gabriel and Alice for a long while until he finally said, "Fine."

"So, Wolverine, what would you like to name him?" Alice asked me.

I thought and thought for a long time until I knew what I wanted to name him. "Niko," I said proudly.

"Niko," she repeated, "That's a great name for a dragon like him. Well, since you named him, he will now be officially yours." Everyone cheered all around me and I was immensely proud. I adore dragons and I would do anything for them. They are especially my favorite.

When everything was over, Gabriel walked over to me and whispered, "You know, Wolverine, that's a pretty fine beast you have here. Are you sure you can deal with him?" he asked me with a nasty little expression on his face.

"Yeah, I think I'll be fine with him," I replied.

"How will you even communicate with him anyway?" he questioned.

"I have my ways and I'll figure it out."

"OK, if you say so." He gave up.

I knew he didn't want me to have Niko, but he knew I had to because it was true what Alice had told him. I needed Niko in every way during my journey. Battling, survival, and comfort. When Gabriel left, I looked at Niko and he looked at me. We both were silent for a moment. I tried getting close to him and he to me as well. Then I tried putting my hand on his nose and he let me. It was such an amazing experience to get along with a beast like this. We both looked at each other in the eye for a second and then, he smiled. I smiled back thinking, *I just made a new friend.*

Since there was an enormous meadow field a mile away from The Two Kingdoms, Niko and I went there to play. It was so much fun. We played and played there until two o'clock. Then I waved at Niko to let him know that I would be leaving. I walked to The Angelic Kingdom to take a breather. As I went into my room, that orb started to get into my head again. I wasn't able to resist the thought, so I took out the box and the key once more, looked at it, but this time I looked at it even harder. Still, nothing. I put everything back underneath the bed at once.

After thirty-five minutes someone knocked on the door. "Yes?" I answered.

This is your mother and the reason why I am here is because you have training with Goliath in five minutes," Alice said.

"Alright, I'll be there," I said.

I went out of my room toward The Demon Kingdom for my last training with Goliath. As I hurriedly walked there, I thought of what Goliath would do for my last day of training with him. To me, I felt like my fighting skills were on point but my survival skills, not that great. When I arrived, Goliath was already waiting for me. When he noticed I'd arrived, he told me I had to follow him to the forest so I could up my skills to know how to survive better.

It took me a while to get used to the forest because I had never really liked the forest. Not because of the animals, such as bears, snakes, or insects. It was because of the dark since you can't see anything when you're in the pitch-black, so you need to have a flashlight in order to see. The problem is, I don't have one, so Goliath would have to teach me how to see through the dark with night vision.

He set the night sky of the forest to nighttime so that my night vision would work. Once he did, he taught me how to use it. It's pretty simple once you get the hang of it. When I got used to having the night vision on there was a challenge that I had to complete. Goliath set the time in the sky for three hours. This was to see if I win if it could increase my skills of survival.

Basically, for those three hours all I had to do was to learn how to find food, stay hydrated, try not to get injured, heal myself, and so on. Since Goliath taught me how to do all those things, I felt like this would be easy-peasy. I was not really nervous but only a little because of course of the dark but also the hunger and my hydration. That was probably why my survival skills were poor but maybe this would help me because surviving a long period of time would increase my ability to survive in the future. Maybe this challenge wouldn't be so bad after all.

"OK, I've set the timer for three hours. When I say go, you will run into the woods as deep as you can go and once you do, try to survive and not come out. Do not worry because if you're hurting badly, I will heal you but other than that, survive. Understood?" Goliath ordered.

"Understood," I responded.

I will count you down in 3 … 2 … 1, *go!*"

I raced through the trees and almost tripped over some rocks but I managed to balance myself. I jumped over some logs, streams, and found a ton of butterflies in the trees. They were very elegant, and one actually landed on my nose. Once I had reached deep into the forest, I wanted to rest so I climbed in a tree to relax. I tried looking for a sturdy type of tree so it wouldn't break. I then spotted a good one, so I climbed it. It was tough because I was tired from all the running I'd done and climbing a tree would be even more tiring. Once I made my way up to a branch that looked like the perfect place to rest, I got settled.

Fifteen minutes passed and I started to get hungry. I thought about some berries but I had to be careful about which ones were safe to eat because I didn't want to get sick only twenty minutes into the challenge, so it was a good thing Goliath had taught me how to sense if anything was poisonous. So, I went in search to find some. I felt like this would be a great start.

Finally, I found some berries on a vine near a stream along a river. The river wasn't so dirty so it would also be good to drink so I could wash the berries too. I sniffed the berries just to make sure and deciding they were ok; I ate some of them and washed them down with water from the river. The water tasted better than I expected it to, so I decided to stay around this area for a while. Plenty of food and water so this would be good for me because I wouldn't have to worry about either.

As I was eating, I was thinking twice about staying here. I couldn't just stay here until the time was up because that wasn't going to help with my survival skills.

In order to build those skills up, I had to go to different parts of the forest. So, once I was done eating, I decided to venture further into the forest to a different location.

I heard movement. Something was running through the trees and the bushes. My heart started racing.

I didn't know what to do so I just stood there, waiting for the creature to reveal itself. As the animal leaped out of the bushes, I squealed until I realized what the animal was.

It was just a bunny!

Chapter 4

Unusual Encounters

All this time I had been feeling nervous for nothing! Maybe it was a good thing I hadn't run. The bunny was ridiculously cute, so I tried slowly petting him. He looked shy but didn't run away. He took a step forward, wanting to trust me and with every step I smiled bigger and bigger. I held out my hands, inviting it to be in my arms.

His fur was white and gorgeous. I picked him up carefully and rubbed him softly, feeling how warm he was. "Hey there, little guy," I said to him. He was very adorable. He then sniffed the air, hard, like something wasn't right. I turned on my night vision so that I could see if something or someone was out there.

The bunny began squeaking nervously and that's when I knew, something wasn't right. The air started to blow hard. I shivered, knowing this wasn't going to be good. I placed the bunny down just in case I needed to run. He went behind my legs, scared. I crossed my arms tightly around me with my knees inward.

My teeth were chattering, and I couldn't stop them. I did not look anywhere else but straight ahead, not even blinking. But when the cold air blew into my eyes, I couldn't help but to blink. That's when a huge tiger pounced. But thanks to my training and night vision, I managed to get out of the way just in time.

The bunny was frightened by the tiger, so he scurried away. The huge tiger swung around, trying to face me. He grinned at me and I was so scared. He was really big. Bigger than any other tiger I'd ever seen. "Stay away from me" I yelled. But he didn't. Instead, he walked toward me, inching closer and closer.

He stopped a good distance from me and said, "You know, I doubt *you* could save your kingdom."

"Excuse me?" I questioned him.

"Well yes, I mean, you don't seem like you could. I'm just saying," he replied.

I was stunned, thinking this could not be happening. "Wait, what? How are you even talking to me right now?" I asked him, confused.

Why was he saying this, and how was he even speaking?

"Tell me, do you know why I are here?" He asked.

"Look," I said, "I don't have time for this. I'm training, and you don't even know that."

"I do," he objected, "but I doubt you would understand why. You're probably still questioning yourself as to why you are even doing this."

"You don't even know if I don't know," I snapped. "Besides, you're just a wild animal, hungry all the time. And actually, why aren't you hurting me right now anyway?"

"I don't want to," he responded casually.

"Then, why approach me?" I challenged him. "You scared me to death when you tried to pounce on me!"

That is true," he chuckled," but I wasn't trying to attack you, Wolverine. I was trying to surprise you!"

"Why, and, how do you even know my name?"

"Number one, because I thought it would be funny and number two, because, well, let's just say, it's been a while."

"Been a while? What do you mean, been a while?" I asked.

"Well, maybe I shouldn't explain. You wouldn't remember, even if I told you," he said.

I squinted at him and then I said, "Fine."

"You know what, now that I'm thinking about it, I think you will be able to save your kingdom," he offered.

"Oh, so *now* you're not doubting me. What made you then?"

"Nothing really, it's just a thought," he said vaguely.

"Right," I said, rolling my eyes, fully annoyed now.

"Anyway, I will be leaving now," announced the tiger.

"Goodbye, Wolverine. Oh and, by the way, the name's Atlas."

As Atlas retreated into the bushes, I watched him suspiciously making sure he wasn't a threat. I looked up from the hill he was on, and he was gone. The air around me started to become still and I wasn't freezing anymore. I wanted to know where the bunny went but I felt like it didn't matter. I kept moving forward to see what else I could discover. I found another stream and decided to see if the water was good to drink. The stream didn't seem to be dirty, so I took a sip of it.

I thought the stream was a good place to camp by, as long as the water was clean to drink and at a good temperature. I wanted to explore other parts of the forest, but then I thought of Atlas. *What if I saw him again?* I wanted to rest on one of the oak trees, so I climbed and sat on a sturdy, thick branch. I crossed my legs, placed my hands in my lap, and rested my head against the bark. Closing my eyes, with a sigh I went to sleep.

I didn't nap for long because a cold splash woke me up. As I looked up at the sky, I realized it was raining, lightning flashed across the sky. In front of me a timer indicated that I had one hour left in the training, which would be good if it wasn't about to storm. I quickly got down from the tree branch in hopes of avoiding lightning strike. I avoided the river because I didn't want to get electrocuted, so I traveled to another area of the forest instead.

I hiked through the trees until I realized I was in a whole different area. Looking around for food and shelter, I found a huge, long, lengthy rope dangling on a branch. As I went to inspect it, I heard a little squeaking sound nearby and it sounded like it was coming from a log that was near me. I went over to look at what was making the sound, and what do you know, it was that same bunny! When he noticed me, he ran toward me, happy to be in my arms again. I was happy too, but not because I found him after such a long time, but because I noticed that he felt safe and protected around me. He was confident and he knew that I wouldn't do him any harm. He trusted me even in the most terrifying situations.

Looking back to the branch, I again felt that something wasn't right. Now looking at it closer, it was bigger than before, and I could see clearer since the rain had kind of stopped. It looked like it had scales with patterns on it. I could see it now; it was not a rope at all. Instead, it was a great, huge tiger snake. That was definitely not good.

I placed the bunny gently inside the log again and told him to stay in there for a bit. The snake stood still, and I wanted to know if it was alive or not, so I threw a rock at it. It woke up immediately. Now knowing that it was alive, it was probably asleep or even maybe it was watching me the whole time. The snake raised its long neck and hissed. I was very startled by it, so I took a step back. The bunny that I told to stay in the log hopped away, for he too, saw the snake.

The snake got closer and closer and with every step towards me, I stepped backwards. He stopped moving and hissed, "Hello."

Did he just talk too? First, the tiger and now this snake! How can this be?

Something was going on and it was not normal. "How am I talking to you right now?" I asked.

"I don't know; how are you?" He hissed once more.

I cocked my head, still wondering what was going on. He was sounding suspicious with all those hissing noises he was making. With a sigh I asked, "Why do you even bother to talk to me anyway? I did hit you with a rock, so I guess you would try to talk some sense into me," I reasoned.

"Well, I could've just taught you a lesson or two, but why do you even bother? You did hit me with that stupid rock of yours during my precious nap! Really, a kid like you would normally have run away by now like a coward. But you, you're not like those fools, are you?" he questioned me back.

"That's because I'm in training," I said, confidently.

"Oh really?" He grinned.

Weirded out by his smirk, I replied, "Yes, I have to train for something very important."

"And, what's that?"

"Don't be so inquisitive, snake! Why does it even matter? It's not something that I can tell a snake like you," I said, sternly.

He chuckled a long chuckle and said, "Well, I already know what you are training for anyway. You're training to kill Ganon, am I right?"

I was taken by surprise. *How did he know that I was going to have to defeat Ganon?*

"Wait, how did you know?"

"Ah, well, should I really be telling you? When I asked what you were training for, you said it was not for snakes so—"

"Not just snakes, snakes like you. Get it right," I corrected him.

The snake growled in his throat but then replied with a grin and continued, "You remind me of your mother. Anyway, what I was saying was, when I asked you what you were training for, you said it was not for snakes *like me*, so why should I tell *you* how I know a human like you?"

"I get your point, but still," I challenged.

"I'm not telling you how I knew. You can beg me all you want but it's not going to spill out. Look, just to end this horrible conversation, how about you just continue on with training or whatever and I, can go back to my lovely nap. So, is it a deal?"

I looked at him doubtfully because I really didn't know if I should trust him. Victoria once told me how snakes represent evil and dangerous creatures. She said that snakes also present as liars and that they are clever, sneaky, and sly. I had a feeling there was something else going on with this snake, like a trick of some sort. "Go on now, don't be shy," he said, this time in a sneaky voice.

"Um … alright," I said anyway. I glanced back at him slowly, watching just to make sure it was safe. Then, I looked forward again and walked back to where I was. But that wasn't smart. He slithered up to me quickly and bit my left ankle. "No!" I screamed in pain. I shook my ankle wildly trying to get him off. But he was too strong, so I tried to get a grip on his tail so I could pull him off, but I then had a better idea. I found a stick laying nearby, so I quickly grabbed a hold of it and threw it at him, which scared him off.

He hissed at me and slunk away into the bushes. I was so relieved that he was gone, but now the pain in my ankle was all I was thinking about. I decided to find a stream or some herbs to heal the bite. I limped through the forest in search of anything that could heal my ankle. Not too far from where I was, I saw a mini waterfall, which I was awfully glad about. I sat on a huge flat rock so I could immerse my foot and ankle in the fresh cold water. It felt so nice and soothing.

Once I was done cleaning my ankle, I was about to grab some herbs and apply some of them to the wound, but it was gone! The painful wound on my ankle was not there anymore.

Is this a miracle? I wondered. *Did the waterfall heal me?*

I tried testing it out again by putting my right hand, which had gotten a cut when I fell, into the water to see if it would heal. When I took my hand out of the water, I waited for a few seconds and then, sure enough, the cut on my right wrist was healed. The cut had vanished and was replaced with new, pure skin!

The waterfall was magical.

But why? Goliath picked a magical forest for me to practice survival!?

This forest was definitely not going to make me improve with water just magically healing up my wounds for me and it was not supposed to, either.

The timer went off signaling the end of my survival training. It was time to return. When Goliath and I walked back to The Two Kingdoms, I decided to ask Goliath about the "magical" forest.

"Goliath, that forest I was training in, it was magical, wasn't it?"

"What do you mean, magical, Wolverine? It's just an ordinary forest," Goliath replied.

"Really?" I said, surprised. "I was talking to animals, and I discovered a magical waterfall."

"Talking to animals and discovering a magical waterfall?" he repeated curiously.

"Yes," I answered. "I was talking to a tiger named Atlas and a snake named, well, he never told me his name, but I was talking to a snake and then he bit me, so I had to find a place where I could clean my ankle. That's when I saw a waterfall, and when I dipped my foot in the water, the wound on my ankle was completely gone in a matter of seconds," I explained.

"Wolverine … what are you talking about? I don't understand," Goliath questioned.

"It is true!" I insisted, wanting him to believe me.

"OK, if you say so. Anyway, Alice said she wants you to go back to your room because she wants you to get a goodnight's sleep before tomorrow."

"OK," I sighed deeply.

As we arrived back at The Two Kingdoms, Goliath said goodbye and announced that he had business to take care of at The Demon Kingdom.

I went up the stairs inside The Angelic Kingdom and went into my room. I jumped and fell backward onto my bed with another deep sigh.

How was that forest not magical? I wondered as I stared at the ceiling.

But wait! Did something happen to *me* that no one else knows?

That's when I knew what it was.

It was that golden orb.

Chapter 5

Wolverine's Journey

It was the morning of the start of my journey, and I had to be up and ready by eight o'clock. The demons at The Demon Kingdom were tidying up Niko for the trip. I went downstairs for breakfast. There were pancakes with syrup and a piece of butter on top. Hash browns and sausages with scrambled eggs galore were to be served hot and ready - anything you would want for a delicious breakfast.

As my stomach couldn't take any more food, it was time to get serious. Alice instructed Niko and I to go into a tech lab that held everything you would need in order to get to Ganon. There was protective gear with weapon-holder belts, weapons, armor, and trackers. A female angel named Sophia gave me a tracker. The tracker showed holograms and warned me of impending danger.

"This, Wolverine, is your tracker," Sophia explained as she placed the gadget on my wrist as if it were a watch. "It will help you along your journey. It will tell you if you're in any danger and alert you to your enemy. It will also let you know where you or Niko are if either of you ever get lost."

I gave her my right wrist so she could put the tracker around it. As the tracker was being placed onto my wrist, I wondered if Niko would be prepared also. "Sophia, is Niko going to get anything special for this journey?"

"Yes, actually," she replied. "Niko will have twice the amount of hearing and smelling. Oh, and not to mention his sight is being upgraded as well. In both of his eyes we are applying two technology lenses so will allow him to zoom in super close."

"Oh, interesting," I said.

"Mmm, hmm! Anyway, there's another angel named Jack and he will show you the ropes for all the weapons and gear you will need. Goodbye, Wolverine, and take care on your journey!" Sophia said excitedly as she waved her hands.

"OK!" I waved back. As I was going to the station where Jack was, my mind was blown. There were so many weapons to choose from. I saw blades, katanas, axes, daggers, and much, much more. It was a good thing Goliath taught me how to use those things. I looked around, searching for a weapon to be claimed as mine until Jack came up to me with a glowing blue sword. "Is that a weapon that I am going to have for my journey?" I asked him.

"One of them," he responded.

"Cool," I said in awe. "What else?"

"Here," he said as he took an axe off a shelf, "this one's pretty heavy but once you get used to it, it will feel as light as air."

"Great!" I said, excitedly, as he handed it to me. I looked around the room of weapons. It was hard to concentrate on just one thing. Everything was so cool and there was so much activity because of the people busily walking around the lab.

"See anything else you want, Wolverine?" Jack asked.

"Erm, no. I think I'm good. I have two weapons," I explained, "and Niko can be my third."

"All right then, that's all I have for you. If you look to your right, you will see another male angel named Skyler. He will outfit you with armor. Good luck!"

All that morning I moved from station to station to get ready. When I was done with each and every station, Alice called Niko and me to her. It was really tense because both Niko and I had epic gear on. Niko looked kind of scary. The lenses that they put on his eyes looked horrifying. His eyes were usually purple, but the lens changed them to a bright orange with only a small pupil in the middle. The armor around his body, legs, and head looked like he could be one of Ganon's guards. I had a feeling that it might take a short while for me to get used to the new Niko.

I didn't know where we were going so, I asked. "So, Alice, where are we going exactly?"

"To Aunt Cornelia," she replied.

"Aunt Cornelia? Who's that?" I further questioned.

"She's the mother of spells and magic," she told me.

"So does that mean she's a witch?" I asked.

"Not technically. But she favors it."

"Oh," I said.

When we arrived at Aunt Cornelia's house, the place was kind of small, but cozy. Outside there was a little fountain, a bird bath, and a small garden located behind her home. She had a big door with a golden sun on it. The house was old and looked like a cottage. When we went inside the tiny home, on the left side there were big spell books with golden suns on them, too.

On the right side of her room were potion bottles lined up neatly in rows on a shelf, and in the back of the room was a fireplace and beside it was a pile of logs. There was a little desk with some pens and ink and a huge spell book. I noticed there was a cauldron in the room, too. "Ah, yes, come in, come in! Is this the Wolverine that I've been waiting to see?" Aunt Cornelia said excitedly.

"Yep, this is her," Alice replied as she smiled proudly.

"Oh, fantastic! Come quickly!"

Aunt Cornelia led Niko and I over to her little desk with the big spell book and started to turn the pages. Everything inside the book looked very ancient. There were a lot of drawings of Greek gods and drawings of how to turn objects into other things. There were even dragons and other creatures too in there. One dragon looked similar to Niko. "There," Cornelia shouted, pointing to something in her spell book that she had found.

"What's that?" I asked her as Alice came over to see what it was too.

"Wolverine, this page will take you somewhere far away from here. This will be the start of your journey. You will travel miles and miles to your destination, and you will not ever turn back. That tracker on your wrist will show you the way to get to Ganon's kingdom. We will all remind you that you are brave, strong, mighty, bold, and best of all, powerful. We all have faith in you, Wolverine, and even your friends. We will miss you," Aunt Cornelia said with a reassuring smile.

"Thank you," I said pleased and honored.

"Now that you have heard my speech, I will now say these magic words that will send you to the jungle," Aunt Cornelia told me. "There is where your journey will begin. And it begins now."

While she spoke the magic words, everything inside the house started to rumble and shake. Then I saw the spell book floating in the air, spinning faster and faster. When Aunt Cornelia said her last words, I closed my eyes, not wanting to be blinded by the strong, giant white light that illuminated from the spell book. When the light faded, I opened my eyes and noticed that Niko and I were in the most beautiful place I had ever seen. There was a little pond with flowers surrounding it not too far away from us.

As I went closer to the pond, I saw my reflection as if I were looking in a mirror. Niko followed, still looking around in amazement. When we were done taking everything in, Niko nudged my arm, trying to tell me something. I tried to understand by watching his movements. "What is it, Niko?" I asked him.

He lay down and nudged his head, trying to point behind him. Now I knew what he wanted. He wanted me to get on his back so he could fly with me! I went over and climbed onto his back. I tried getting a grip on him before we lifted off. He spread out his wings and then zoomed off the ground. He went so fast; I didn't think I would be able to hold on. He went high into the air like an airplane flying high above the white, fluffy clouds. Niko then slowed down, sensing that I needed to catch my breath and enjoy the beautiful scenery from below. It was very peaceful.

I looked at my tracker to see where we were going next. It seemed kind of close. The next destination was some type of poor, small town. It looked desert-like. I decided to tell Niko about it. "Niko, my tracker says that if you keep flying straight ahead, we will arrive at a new area and it looks like it's in a desert. Some type of ghost town desert."

He made a raptor-like sound that sounded like, "OK."

After a thirty-five-minute flight we approached our destination. In the distance I saw a little town with barely any buildings. Niko dived through the clouds toward the small town. My ears were popping on the way down. The almost baren place had houses that looked like tiny huts. When we landed and got settled, I jumped off Niko's back and walked toward the town. People noticed me with Niko, and they were scared and horrified. They were also frightened because I had weapons on me. As I was walking, the people kept moving back, letting me through.

I then saw a tall, mean-looking female elf walking toward me. Niko made a little whining sound and ducked his head behind me. When she stopped, she said, "Who are you, and why are you here?" Her tone sounded so stern.

I was trembling because I didn't know what to say or to do. She looked tough and looked like she would beat me up any second now. She was so tall! "I'm here because I have to do something very important," I responded.

"And that is?" She continued to question be sternly.

"I have come from a kingdom not too far from here," I reported. "It is called The Two Kingdoms. My parents, Alice and Amorok, sent me here to destroy something in this town."

"To destroy something here. What is there to destroy? There's nothing here! Just our homes! Who are you! AND SAY IT LOUD," she yelled.

"My name is Wolverine Amirith!" I reply with all my might.

She winced her eyes at me like she was trying to remember something. "You!? Your parents have been making us suffer here! They cursed and kept us in misery here in this desert place! Your parents are nothing but fools! They punished us! I don't believe that you will help us. You will just make it worse for us!" She was very upset.

It scared me how loud she was. From behind I could hear Niko growling like he wanted to do something. "Why did my parents do that? There had to be something you did wrong," I challenged.

She sighed and looked back at her people, then back at me. "I'll tell you what happened. Long, long ago, we lived in a beautiful environment filled with trees, livestock, and peace. Everything there was an eternity of peacefulness, and it still is. But one day, an evil spirit came and told us an evil, evil lie. It told us that there existed a kingdom a long way from here, saying that there lived a baby and the baby lived at that kingdom. It was called The Two Kingdoms. Now, here's the lie the evil spirit told us. It told us that if we stole the baby, we would never have to worry about peace and that everyone would have the knowledge of good and evil. So, we agreed to set off into the night to steal the baby. But then we got caught by the guards at The Angelic Kingdom and your parents punished us for it. So, the best thing they could think of to punish us with, was to live in this place, forever!"

"Well, you deserved it," I said.

"Deserved it?! Did your parents raise you to have understanding? That evil spirit *made* us!" She confronted.

"No, it didn't. You chose to. All of you did. That evil spirit informed you about it," I explained. "But you made the choice."

Some of the people were nodding in agreement and the woman noticed. She looked kind of sad, but also mad.

"Alright," she sighed, "I guess you are right about that."

"Anyway, like I said, there's one thing I have to destroy here."

"What's that?" She murmured.

"Is there a type of monster that has been lurking around here?" I asked.

"Actually, yes, there is. It has haunted us here for decades. Is that what you're going to destroy here?"

"Yes," I replied. "Don't worry, ma'am. I have been trained and I know all sorts of things, including how to fight."

"Well, OK. But I'll have to warn you about something," she said, concerned.

"What is it?" I questioned, prepared to hear what she had to say.

"This monster is a god, known as the Sand God. He is really powerful, and he terrorizes us. Some of my people have tried to destroy him but we failed and a lot of us died, so we stopped trying. Are you sure you can handle him?"

"Oh, definitely," I said confidently. "Niko and I know how to handle him."

"OK. So, I guess I'll have to show you where he lives."

She walked Niko and me to what I think is one of the scariest places I have ever seen. There was nothing here! Just sand and, more sand. The sky became dark green and black, more of a zombie-like color. But I didn't see the monster that I had to destroy.

"So, this is the place?" I asked her.

"Yep, this is it," she replied.

I kept looking and looking and I still couldn't find it. Then, I felt a rumble under my feet and then something jumped up from under the sand. It was a giant mega worm with huge teeth. Good thing I was ready because when it jumped, I took out my glowing blue sword in a flash and slashed the worm in the neck. It fell to the ground with a loud, enormous thud and a roar.

"That's the monster?!" I questioned in horror.

"Well, yes, you said that you wanted to defeat it, didn't you?" She asked.

"Yes, but I never imagined it would be this huge!" I admitted.

"Trying to imagine in the mind won't help to unsee the reality. Anyhow, good luck with the battle."

She disappeared in the air and I looked at Niko. He was having a hard time with the worm, so I joined in the fight to help him out. I'd learned about these things before. It was in an old book that talked about different types of creatures and one of the chapters talked about the worm. But I didn't understand it fully because it was written in an unfamiliar language. I could only understand the pictures.

I used my sword to inflict some nice damage. It helped well with the battle. Niko caused some pretty nice damage as well. I made some moves that seemed a little scary and dangerous, but I was careful to perform the right moves at the right time.

The worm became weak and fell to the side. With every inch of movement he made, he would roar. To end the fight, I decided to stab the worm in the eye with my axe. The worm's eye was really big so I knew that I would have to hit it right in the center of it. As he lay there, unable to get up, I stabbed him with the axe and then, he was gone, instantly.

After the fight, we went back to the town to share the news. As we arrived and began telling the people, they didn't believe me and stated that I only said that because I didn't want them to be scared. I tried to convince them, but they refused to listen. Then, a flash of light came down toward me and went into my body. Well, that caused them to believe me since apparently that sort of thing only happened when you defeat a god.

The people were stunned. They looked like they didn't want to believe that they saw what happened, but they knew what they saw, and they couldn't unsee it again. "Well," I started to say, "how 'bout that. Now do you believe me?" I was ready for an answer.

They all nodded their heads, slowly, still in shock and disbelief. Then the tall lady came to me and smiled. That was the first time I'd seen a smile from her since Niko and I arrived. Gosh!

"Well," I said, "I defeated your monster, happy?"

"Very," she exclaimed with excitement. "I thought that monster would never die since none of my people have ever been able to do it. How did you even do it?" She asked in awe of me.

"Well, it's not just about how powerful you are or how many people you're fighting. It's about not giving up on yourself and fighting for a cause. Most importantly, it is about always believing in yourself so that one day you will achieve something that will help others by making the right decisions." As I stopped speaking, I realized the woman's face was smiling the biggest smile I had ever seen. So, I smiled too!

"Well," she began, "since you've defeated the monster, how about we all celebrate you for it."

"Really? You don't have to," I said.

"Oh, please? We would love to appreciate you for your hard work. Killing that monster and sharing your secret has left us so inspired, so we just want to thank you. I'm sorry I was being so rude to you and your dragon friend earlier. I was just so scared. But I understand you better now. Please celebrate with us," she begged.

I looked at her for a while because I really didn't have the time to congratulate myself and to spend time with her and the people to celebrate my victory of the monster that I slayed. "I'm sorry, ma'am, but Niko and I don't have the time for a celebration right now. I have an important journey ahead of me. I have to succeed. I have to destroy Ganon," I explained.

"Ganon? You know about him?" She asked me.

"Yes," I replied. "He's trying to destroy my kingdom so, my parents sent me off on a quest to defeat him."

"Uh! He's so evil! I once had to speak with him not too long ago," she revealed.

"Really? How long was that?" I asked.

"About two weeks ago, actually."

"Why did he want to speak with you?" I said, wanting to find out more about the situation.

'I-I can't tell you."

"Why not?"

"It's private. Only Ganon and I can talk about this," she answered.

"What's wrong with telling me?" There was something fishy going on. I did not like the idea of her keeping some secret between her and Ganon. I decided to keep pushing.

"Nothing. But it's best to keep it that way. That's what Ganon told me," She said.

"Why would you do what Ganon tells you to do? I wouldn't let him be the boss of me," I said.

"You know how foolish he is, and, if I don't keep it a secret, you would share it. And I don't want it to get to the point where everyone knows about it. If he finds out, he might punish us to suffer even more and—"

"If you share it with me, I promise not to share it with everyone else. I would never do that."

She looked at me with such fear in her eyes. I knew she was scared but I wanted to make her comfortable sharing the secret. I wanted her to trust me and not worry about anything she may share.

"You know what, you're right. I do trust you with all of my heart and I know you would never share with anyone about it. So, I will tell you what Ganon and I discussed."

"OK," I said, relieved she was going to tell me the secret.

"The reason why there's a secret between me and Ganon is because I work for him. The reason for this, is because he wanted to make a deal with me and the people. He said that he would provide us with everything we needed if I work for him. Before all of this happened, I'd heard about how evil he was, and I didn't want my people and I to be involved with him, but it was the only way we wouldn't have to suffer as much. So, I agreed to the deal he made. When I made the deal, I told myself that I would always remember the grin he had on his face. It was the evilest grin I had ever seen. After the agreement, his last words were to keep the secret between him and me. Then he left."

"Wow. You couldn't even tell your people?"

"Nope," she replied. I didn't want them to be worried or scared."

"I know what you mean," I said understandingly. After our talk, I told her I would have to leave.

"Wait," she stopped me. "Just to let you know, my name is Oleana."

"OK, thank you for telling me, Oleana," I said as I waved my hand to say goodbye.

I went to get on Niko's back and together we rode into the sunset to find a place to sleep.

Chapter 6

It Felt So Real

I saw a light coming from a candle up on a wall leading to a giant door in front of me in a hallway. I looked around, trying to see where I was. I was wondering why I was here, and Niko wasn't. It was all very strange to me. There wasn't much in the hallway but the door in front of me. To find out more information about where I was, the only option was to go through the door.

I opened the door slightly, not wanting to bust in first. I saw two figures dressed in red and black. Their conversation sounded like an argument. I decided to keep spying. Maybe I could get something from their conversation.

"Tydus! When is it done?!" One asked.

"It still has a long way to go, Your Highness. I'm sorry, but you're going to have to wait a little longer," Tydus replied.

"I don't have time to wait much longer, Tydus, and you know that! Wolverine is going to *destroy* us if we don't get that thing under control! This is serious!" The one Tydus referred to as Your Highness reminded him.

"Yes, I know that you're impatient, Your Highness, but the only way it will be finished sooner is if you're patient." Tydus released a tired sigh.

"OK, fine, you know what? Just bring her over to me now and leave. Got that?"

"Yes sir, Your Highness," Tydus said.

As he went to open the door, I panicked. *What was happening?*

What did that person yelling at that guy named Tydus want from me? He wasn't even really a human, he was just some scary looking half human, half monster. Tydus opened the door and motioned for me to come to him. Reluctantly, I did.

"OK, Wolverine, come with me," Tydus ordered.

"Um … why?" I questioned without moving.

"The king wants to have a discussion with you," he replied.

"Why does he want to speak with me?"

"Reasons," he replied vaguely. "Now come."

I followed him and to be honest I'd never been more terrified. There were times I had been really scared, but I was thinking this was one of the most horrifying things I had ever done. I had no idea who that creature was that was yelling at Tydus. After Tydus delivered me as he had been instructed, he left and went on his way without saying more.

"Well … Wolverine, I'm glad you are here," the half monster, half human announced in a loud and bold tone. He looked at me like he was staring into my soul.

"Um, yeah, I guess. Erm, who are you?" I asked, trying to sound braver than I felt.

"Do you need to ask? My name is Ganon," he answered.

"Wait, what?"

"Well, of course, who else would it be?"

To his reply I rolled my eyes. I couldn't believe *this* was Ganon. I never knew I was going to meet him so soon! But I did. "I've heard so much about you. Everyone told me you are like an evil monster," I told him.

"I know. Thank you for your compliment!" He smiled proudly.

"That wasn't a compliment," I said flatly.

"Whatever," he said dismissively. "But there's a reason why you're here, Ms. Amerith," he confessed with a secret grin on his face that was barely visible.

"Oh, and what is that?" I asked.

"It's a plan that I have been working on for quite a while now."

"Is it the plan that you and that guy named Tydus were babbling about?" I asked.

"Yes, and there's nothing you can do about it," he told me.

71

"You don't know how powerful I am, Ganon," I reported.

"Oh, but I do know that I am definitely more powerful than you. Listen, Wolverine, I've had my eyes on you ever since your 'friends' told you the story of our history. I've been listening to every single word that came out of your mouth and to be honest, I hadn't minded at all."

"So, basically, you're saying that you were stalking me?" I questioned him.

"Yep," he replied without shame or remorse.

"Of course, you would," I muttered.

"But there's just one small problem," he confessed.

"I'm listening," I said, doubting this would be good.

"I've heard you talking to Oleana about the secret I share with her. I knew I shouldn't have trusted her. Later, she will regret it," he warned.

"What are you going to do?" I asked. "Are you going to hurt her?"

"Don't you worry about that," he replied. "I have my ways. More important to me than that is this, I need to ask you something."

"What is—"

"Your Highness, we found a trespasser in our kingdom." Tydus interrupted as he quickly approached us.

Ganon sighed under his breath angrily and asked, "Who is it?"

"It's a woman. She is with the guards," Tydus replied.

Ganon sighed again and said, "I'll attend to that matter now. You stay here and guard Wolverine. She *cannot* leave while I'm gone. Understood?"

"Understood, Your Highness," replied Tydus.

Ganon left and silence about the room making it awkward to even bear a word. When I was about to say something, Tydus beat me to it, "So, we meet again?"

"Uh, yeah, we have," I replied. More silence and I had no idea what to say until a question popped up in my head. "Who is the woman trespassing?"

"Oh, the woman? I don't know. She might have come from a village to spy on us or something. That's what I think."

"Oh," I said.

Tydus looked at me but then back at something else. I did the same thing. Then, he looked back at me and said, "You're wondering why you're here, aren't you?"

"I looked at him and answered, "Yeah, I'm confused. I don't understand what's happening. I'm not sure if this is real or fake. And hey, who are you anyway?"

Tydus looked at me with a sad expression on his face and said, "Another time I will tell you."

"Another time? How do you know if I'm going to be able to see you again?" I asked.

"I'll tell you everything, when the time comes," he repeated.

I cocked my head wondering what in the world he was talking about.

"Actually, since Ganon hasn't come back yet, do you want to leave?" He asked me.

"Leave? Didn't he want you to guard me so I *couldn't* leave?''

"I don't do everything Ganon tells me to do. So, now's your chance. Do you want to leave?"

I hesitated for a moment thinking that this was a joke, but from the look on Tydus's face I could tell that he really wanted to help me. Then I said, "Yes, I want to leave."

Out of nowhere, I awoke to the feel of soft grass under me. I sat up quickly wondering where I was now, until I remembered this was the place where Niko and I decided to rest. I looked around and saw Niko already awake resting beside a tree, waiting for me to wake up.

As I thought about what had just happened, I learned that it was all just a dream.

Why was I dreaming about Ganon and Tydus? What did it mean? There had to be a reason for the dream, right?

I knew it was a message, but I just couldn't quite understand it. I went toward Niko. "I'm awake, Niko. You were growing impatient waiting for me to get up, weren't you?" I said as I pet his nose. He growled softly in his throat as if to say, "It's alright." He then got up and stretched his legs. Then he ducked his nose to the ground and then into the air. "What is it, Niko?" I questioned him. He then started to sniff the ground even more. Then, he trotted along into the forest, while sniffing. "Hey, wait up," I yelled. I wanted to find out what he was smelling.

Was he smelling something dangerous? Or was he smelling something weird? Or even maybe something delicious?

As I made my way through the trees, I saw a little black and white creature looking like it was still in slumber. I knew it wouldn't be long before he woke up though.

"A skunk? Niko, were you smelling a skunk?" I asked him.

He didn't reply back but instead he went closer the skunk. And then closer. I tried going in front of him so he wouldn't be interested. He nudged my body away so I tried something different. I tried pushing him aside, but he was too heavy to even budge. He was just so fascinated by the skunk. "Look, dragon. There are more important things to discover than the skunk."

Niko looked at me then back at the skunk. Then he made a little grunting noise as if to say, "Fine, you're right," and went along to somewhere else.

I followed him, wanting to see where he was going next. He stopped at a nearby tree and started scratching himself. Oh great, I followed him for nothing. So, I tried going to explore things on my own. But when I went, Niko noticed me and followed along too.

We stopped nearby a cave that appeared to be empty, so I decided to explore it. Niko was sniffing the whole area while I tried to find what was in there. When I found nothing and thought of leaving instead, Niko, nudged my left arm. "What is it, Niko?"

He showed me the way to a yellow light luminating from underneath the ground. I went to see what it was, and I realized it was another golden orb just like the one I found under my bed.

But where did this one come from?

I picked it up and tried to do the same thing I did with the other. This time, the orb changed to a purple color. "Niko, what do you think this orb means?" I questioned him.

"I'm not sure," he responded.

I couldn't believe it. Niko was talking too! I knew the power of the orbs. The orbs allowed me to talk to certain types of animals. Different color orbs allowed me to talk to different animals. I guessed the yellow orbs allowed me to talk to forest-like animals while the purple orbs allowed me to talk to mystical-type creatures.

This was huge for me. I'd successfully figured out the mystery of the orbs. "Niko," I smiled joyfully, "you can talk?!"

"I can?" He looked at me, then back at himself. He seemed confused, but equally amazed. "But how?"

"Niko, it is all because of the purple orb!" I laughed.

Chapter 7

Who Are You?

Niko looked at the glowing purple orb that was in my hands in amazement. He went in for a closer look. "That thing can make me talk?" He asked me, still looking down at the orb.

"Niko, I don't think the orb made you have the power to speak. I think it made *me* have the power to communicate with creatures just like you as well as other types of mystical creatures. Because on one of my days of training, I was talking to a tiger and a snake."

"But Wolverine, tigers and snakes aren't magical creatures. They're just forest-like animals," corrected Niko.

"You're right. In my room one day I found a little box and inside that box was a yellow orb. That was the first time I'd seen one of these orbs. The yellow orbs must allow me to speak with forest-like animals," I reasoned.

"Oh. So, why do they exist? What's the point of them?"

"That's what I kind of want to know too, Niko," I admitted.

While Niko and I were discussing the orb's power, a huge figure appeared. The figure didn't make a noise while it walked, but the shadow it cast told us it was definitely a large being. The shape looked strangely familiar, like someone or something I'd seen before.

"So, we meet again," the familiar voice said.

I squinched my eyes attempting to see through the dark fog the image had cast upon us. I was sure I had seen this animal before. But I knew I wouldn't get a good guess through the heavy, thick fog. Niko made a loud growl in his throat. As the shadow became clear to us, I could see him now. It was Atlas, again. I had no idea this cave was his home. This cave was huge and quite likely suited him well.

"You know, Wolverine, it is kind of rude to invade someone's territory while they are away," he informed me.

"Oh, Atlas, I-I didn't know this was your home," I responded apologetically.

"Say, why are you and your friend here?" He asked.

"Um, well, Niko and I just found a purple orb. We discovered that this particular orb gives me the power to speak with magical creatures," I told him.

Atlas looked at the orb, then back at me again. "So, you finally found one. Your first orb."

"Huh? No, no, no. This is actually the second orb I've found. There was one under my bed in The Angelic Kingdom," I told confessed.

"Really? Interesting. Anyway, I guess you should be going on your way now since that's what your mission is, ay?" He urged.

"Yeah, I guess. C'mon, Niko," I said. Niko made a grunt noise as if saying, "OK," instead of speaking it aloud. After that, we left.

Atlas was mysterious. In my mind it felt like he wasn't just an ordinary tiger. I reflected on our first encounter during my initial training session in the forest. "Niko, doesn't Atlas look like he could be mischievous?" I asked.

"Who's Atlas?" Niko asked as he locked his eyes somewhere else.

"That tiger, Niko! Didn't you hear me say his name?"

"Oh yeah, right. I was focused on something else," he said absently.

I sighed and said, "I know this is your first time seeing him. But, since you've experienced him now, aren't you thinking about him the same way? Don't you notice how suspicious he is?"

Niko looked back to see if he was still there, but Atlas was gone. "Huh, where did he go?"

"It's odd, isn't it, Niko?" I asked.

"Yeah, and it's weird how he does that. You're right, Atlas is only suspicious, he is weird too," he agreed.

"And look! The orb's gone too!" I realized.

"Do you think he took it with him?"

"Probably. I doubt that he wouldn't. Anyway, let me check my tracker so we can see where to go next," I told him.

"OK, but first can we eat something because I'm *super* hungry right now!" Niko groaned.

"OK, OK, Niko, we'll get food. Just, chill out and be patient, will you?" We started out in the forest to find some fruit. After the search, we found plenty and decided to rest near a pond to eat. It was delicious!

After our meal Niko and I continued to our next mission. Niko waited for me to get on his back and together, we flew into the air. I looked on my tracker and it said we were going into some kind of a spooky forest.

When we got there, the forest was foggy and cold. The wind quietly whispered through my ears. Here, everything was quiet. Niko was confused.

"Are you sure this is the right location because it doesn't seem like this is where we should be."

"It has to be," I replied. "I'm looking at my tracker right now and it's still showing the same location."

"Well, then maybe it's broken," he suggested.

Then, I heard something shake through the nearby trees. I saw a figure walking around, slowly. I alerted Niko immediately. "Niko, do you see that?"

"See what?" Niko asked.

"That figure over there!"

Niko looked in the direction where I pointed, and his eyes went wide.

"Maybe I'll look closer. Just to see what that shadow thing is," I suggested.

"Be careful, Wolverine, it kind of looks like a monster. I don't want you to get hurt," he said worriedly.

"Don't worry, I'll be fine," I said, assuring him.

I walked ten steps toward the figure until I accidently stepped on a twig. My heart stopped as I saw the figure facing me. I yelled for Niko to run, and we ran as fast as we could away from the strange figure.

A voice I found so familiar called out to me. "Hey!" I could hear its footsteps after me, so I tried to run faster. When I was out of breath and couldn't hear any more footsteps, I told Niko that we could stop.

Then, out of nowhere, I saw a beast with wings fly down right in front of me. He scared the wits out of me. It had been Tydus all along. I sighed in relief, thinking it was someone or something else. His face looked serious and sad. I could tell he was down about something.

"Tydus, why did you have to scare me like that? You nearly gave me a heart attack!"

"I was trying to find you. I thought you might be here. I have to tell you something because my time is running out and this is especially important. I know I was weird and all

when you were at Ganon's kingdom, and there's just
something I need to tell you."

Before I could say anything, Niko blurted out at Tydus.
"YOU," Niko screamed.

That scared me. "Niko, what are you yelling at him about?
Do you know him?"

"Yes, I know him!" Niko replied. "He's Ganon's 'special'
assistant who always made fun of me! Me, out of all the
other dragons, who was being held hostage. I would be the
one who would get bullied the most and it wasn't fair!
Wolverine, he is nothing but a joke!"

I looked at Tydus. His face was changing to more of a pale
color. But for some reason I could tell he was sad about
something else and that he was very confused. Then he said
to Niko, "I have no idea what you're talking about."

Niko started to get angrier and angrier. "Yes, you do! You
know you do. You've heard me talk about how cruel you
were to me to her, didn't you? You can't just lie to her like
that when I'm literally four feet away from you! You think
you can be slick like that, you snake!?"

"Hey! Look! I wasn't lying!" Tydus yelled back furiously.

"Yes, you are!" Niko shouted. "We saw that face you made
at her!"

"I wasn't making that face because of that, crazy!" Tydus
said visibly frustrated.

"Then for what reason? I want to hear an explanation, pronto!" I had never seen Niko so upset.

"Hey! Both of you chill!" I strictly ordered them. They both immediately stopped to face me, shocked. "Niko, did you really have to lose your cool like that?" I asked him.

"He needed to understand that he's not as cunning as he thinks he is!" He told me.

"OK, but if you argue, it will not help the situation. Couldn't you at least let me deal with it instead?" I asked.

He looked at Tydus, then at me, then at the ground. "Fine."

"Good," I said. After Niko agreed, I looked at Tydus. "Tydus, what is the important thing you wanted me to know?"

"I was trying to tell you in Ganon's kingdom that there *would* be a time when I would see you again when the time was right. I know that it was weird. But what I wanted to tell you was—"

"Wait, before you tell her about that part, can you please explain to us about why you are here? I mean, I knew it was because of Wolverine, but first of all, how did you *know* we would be here?" Niko asked.

"I hacked her tracker," Tydus confessed.

Silence hushed us, then Niko said, "OK, well that explains it. The main question I had was, was there another reason why you're here?"

Tydus sighed and said, "Yes. There was something here that Ganon wanted so he made me come look for it."

"Why couldn't he just find it for himself, instead of sending you?" Niko asked.

"Because like you said, I am his assistant and that's what assistants do," he said quietly.

"But still."

"Can I please tell Wolverine something important! I let you speak so now it is my turn to speak, thank you very much!" Tydus said, annoyed again.

"Fine, whatever makes you happy," Niko replied curtly.

After Tydus let out a short sigh, he continued, "Look, Wolverine, you're in serious danger and it's worse than what it seems."

"Why are you telling me this, Tydus? Why do you even bother to care? You said you're working for Ganon, aren't you?" I asked.

"Yes, but I've been waiting about trying to have this conversation with you. So, can you bear with me?"

"I'll try my best," I promised.

"A long time ago, I used to live at The Two Kingdoms. There, I was just an innocent demon like the rest of the demons there. The only thing different about me from the rest was that I had a secret. A secret that was so powerful. The secret was this; I had almost as much power as Ganon. No one knew until Ganon somehow found out. I didn't know how, for I never did anything that needed such power. When Ganon discovered my power, he decided to use me for his plan. He made a deal with me that I found impossible to say no to. When I agreed for him to test me, the results left him shocked."

"Why did the results shock him?" I questioned.

"He realized that I wasn't the only one who had my power, according to the results," he answered.

"Then, who?" I questioned, uncertain I wanted to know.

"You're not going to believe this but the power I have is the same as Queen Alice, King Amorok, Aunt Cornelia, and even you!" Tydus declared.

"Wait. Alice and Amorok are my parents! How is that possible then?" I asked, confused.

"Try to figure it out," he said.

"OK, well, if they have the same power as you, then that means that you must have the same blood as my family."

"Correct," he nodded.

"And if you have the same blood as my parents and I, then you would have to be related."

"Mm-hmm, keep going."

"So, if you're related to my parents, does that mean you're their son!?" I interrogated.

"Yep. But you're missing one more thing," he said.

"OK, well, if you're the son, then that makes me the daughter?"

"Right …" he coaxed.

"And if I'm the daughter that means … I'm your sister."

"And I'm your brother."

I stared at him a long time. I was shocked. It did make sense. We looked a little bit similar. Niko was not pleased with this. I'm sure he thought this was a trap that Ganon set. My suspicions were quickly confirmed.

"Wolverine, this is all a trap!" Niko warned.

"Niko, how can you be so sure?" I asked him.

"You know he's almost as much a trickster as Ganon. This is all just Ganon's doing right here!" He said completely convinced.

"But—" I stopped. I thought for a long time.

Could Tydus really be messing with me?

"Tydus, is this really true? Are you really my brother?" I pressed.

"Positive. As my sister, I would never lie to you," he replied, sad faced.

"Liar," Niko quickly added.

Tydus started to get really annoyed now. "It's true! I am her brother!"

"If you're her brother, why are you still working for that Ganon, huh? That's not what a brother does for their sister!"

"That's one reason why I am here to tell Wolverine this! I had to tell her now that I'm not working for Ganon anymore!"

After that last sentence, he disappeared with a *poof*. Niko stood frozen. I stood frozen. Even the area we were in stood frozen. Niko faced me and said, "Where'd he go?"

I gave no reply. Instead, I just said, "Let's go." I looked down at the ground with a long sigh. I wasn't sad about the fact that Tydus and Niko were arguing. Well, a little bit. But I was mostly sad about the fact that he would really confront Ganon about quitting. For me.

As Niko and I walked for a bit, Niko stopped in front of me and said, "Look, I'm sorry for what happened back there. I guess I was overreacting a bit about Tydus. Maybe he was actually really serious."

"Yeah," I said.

"I know you're mad at me right now but, can you please forgive me? Everyone makes mistakes, right? Even dragons make mistakes."

"Niko, I forgive you. You can forget about your worries. I know you were only trying to look out for me, that's all," I said.

"Yeah, thanks for understanding. And hey, was there anything you were dreaming about when we were sleeping? I'm just wondering."

My heart stopped. "Actually, uh, yeah," I replied.

"What were you dreaming about?" He asked.

This question made me really tense up. I remembered that dream was really something. I hardly knew what it really meant. "Oh, it was kind of confusing."

"Really, how? Who was in your dream?"

I hesitated for a long time because I was too nervous to tell him. I didn't know why but I just was. Finally, I managed to get the name out. "Ganon," I said, sighing hard.

Niko almost lost his balance, but I somehow helped steady him just at the right moment. Don't forget he is really heavy. When he was standing upright again, he froze in shock. "Not Ganon."

"Yep," I answered.

"Describe what he looks like so I confirm for you if that was the real Ganon."

"He has dark red fur, he stands about seven and a half feet, has dark red colored eyes, black and red clothing, and he has a very deep and bold voice," I described.

"Yep, that's him. Who else was in your dream, Tydus?" he asked.

"Yes," I reply.

"Of course."

"Niko, I have a question for you now. What were you talking about when you said there were other dragons that were held hostage?" I asked.

"Oh, that? Ganon right now is using dragons to help him with his plan. I was one of them, until Ganon kicked me out because I wasn't that powerful. He kicks dragons out that aren't powerful. That's how that angel named Gabriel found me. I was simply in an open area, lost and with nowhere to go."

"Man, well, Niko, I think that dream I had was like a message. Throughout the entire thing, I couldn't comprehend it, nor could I understand it. But I do remember the talk me and Ganon had, and something wasn't really right about him. When he was speaking, it's almost as if he couldn't stop looking at the spell book that was a little way away from us. It was the same spell book Aunt Cornelia had as well. All of this just doesn't make sense to me at all," I explained.

"Wolverine, you saw that spell book?"

"Yes," I replied.

"Well, you're not going to believe all this," he said, scared.

"What is it?" I asked, worried.

"OK, so, Aunt Cornelia has the same spell book that Ganon has, right? They're actually multiple copies of those that you can earn from trials. Now, here's the part where I alleviate your confusion. Do you remember anything in that spell book that you saw when Aunt Cornelia was flipping through those pages?"

"I saw a dragon that looked like you," I guessed.

"Something else."

"A weird looking skull?" I guessed again.

"More?"

"A silvery white-looking gem?"

"BINGO!" he yelled out. "That silvery white-looking gem that you saw in that spell book is the central issue to all your problems. It's what Ganon wants."

"Wait. Why does Ganon need that? What does it do?" I asked.

"Wolverine, Ganon thinks that you have it. That's all I know," he said.

"Huh? Why would he think that I, the daughter of The Two Kingdoms, would have it?"

"Someone told him that you had it. That was probably the reason why he had that meeting with you. He wanted to know if *you* had it," he explained.

"Erm, I don't know about that. Besides, he never asked me if I had the gem. All he ever said was that he had a plan to destroy me once and for all."

"Maybe it's because he hasn't gotten to that part yet," Niko said, trying to make a point.

"Maybe," I said. "And hey, how do you know about all this?"

"My horns are the key. They tell me information about what others are saying. They can even comprehend books that are in a different language. That's one reason why Ganon needed us dragons, so he could understand different languages. And also, I had a friend there who would tell me Ganon's plans. He was Ganon's favorite."

"Niko, in the dream I had about Ganon, he didn't really tell me what his plan actually was. Do you know?" I asked.

"Yes, but I have to warn you, Wolverine, it's a very smart plan. You should be grateful I am telling you this."

"Yes, very," I said. "Now tell me."

"His plan requires traps along the route of your journey. But there was one trap he knew you got caught into, way before your journey started. It was when it was your last day at training. Do you remember anything that tried to attack you?" Niko asked me.

"During my training in the forest I saw a big tiger snake. It did attack me!" I said angrily, remembering the pain in the place where he bit.

"That snake is Ganon's helper, and pet. He is well known as Synthus, that is his name. He is also well known to be mostly as evil as Ganon," he explained to me.

"How did Ganon know I was going to be in that specific forest?" I asked him.

"There's a big, white, crystal-like globe he has and every day he tracks you."

"Oh yeah, Amorok was talking about that once. Anyway, we should keep going with our mission. We're wasting our time figuring out different things when really we should be focusing on our main mission," I reminded Niko.

"You're right," Niko agreed. "Hop on my back."

I hopped onto his back and together, we flew to our next location.

Chapter 8

The Creepy Mansion

We arrived at an enchanted forest just like the tracker directed. There, we saw different colors and sizes of mushrooms that were spread all over the forest. I could see fairies there too. They were almost my size.

But there was one thing that really caught my eye. At the back of the forest was a big creepy mansion. I remembered I was sitting on a sidewalk reading a book about the old mansion. I didn't really understand it too much, though; the only thing I knew about it was that a young girl lives there. The old mansion caused shivers down my spine. I decided to not think about it too much and approached the fairies. One was blue and the other was purple. Niko followed along, slowly.

"Hi, excuse me?" I said. The fairies turned around quickly. "Oh, I'm sorry that I scared you both—"

"It's fine," the blue fairy interrupted, enthusiastically. "And who are you both?"

I hesitated for a split second and replied, "My name is Wolverine, and this is Niko."

They looked at each other with big smiles on their faces. Then they looked back at us. "It's you! You're the one Aunt Cornelia told us about!" The purple fairy said excitedly.

I was surprised. How did they know about her? "Wait, how do you about Aunt Cornelia?" I asked them.

The blue one replied, "We fairies here in this forest are her helpers. Whether she needs a type of book at our library or any type of samples of potions she may want to try out, it's all hers."

"Wow," I said, "I never knew that Aunt Cornelia had helpers. So, that's where all those books and potions she has come from. It just comes from here, right?"

"Indeed!" The blue one confirmed. "We've helped her for a long time."

"By the way," I said. "What are your names?"

They both looked shocked. "Oh! We're sorry!" The purple one giggled. "We haven't even introduced ourselves yet. My name is Blooma."

"And my name's Hazel!" The blue one said.

"Also," Blooma started, "Aunt Cornelia said that you were coming here to help us with our troubles."

"Yes, I have. What are your troubles?" I asked her.

"Do you see that mansion at the back of this forest? That part is called the Dark Woods. There, lives a girl named

Aveline and a dragon named Porcupine," Blooma explained.

"Porcupine?" I asked, confused.

"That's what Aveline calls him. The dragon is her pet," Hazel explained.

"Oh. What type of dragon is it?"

"A night dragon," Blooma answered.

"He's very scary," Hazel told us.

"I can imagine," I said.

"Anyway," Blooma said, "Aveline never comes out of the mansion because she doesn't want to leave Porcupine. She really loves him. But the dragon is dangerous. He pretends to love her for his mind is like that of a trickster."

"So, he's a trickster-type dragon?" I asked.

"And a mind-controlling dragon," Hazel added.

"Yes, and a mind-controlling dragon," Blooma repeated. "What he does is he tricks and mind-controls the girl. Though poor Aveline, she doesn't notice it."

"What should I do then to help her?" I asked.

"Two things," said Hazel. "One, you have to make Aveline believe Porcupine is evil. Two, once she believes you, you will have to kill him."

"I guess I can do that," I lied, thinking that would be impossible to do.

"Farewell!" Blooma.said.

"Good luck!" Hazel chimed in.

As Niko and I trotted along to the mansion, the forest became darker and darker until we could hardly see anything but the lights on in the mansion. The lights weren't helping to see through the darkness, so I decided to use the night vision Goliath taught me. As I slowly walked toward the door, I steadily knocked on it. The door seemed heavy when I banged on it. Behind the door I could hear the voice of a young girl, "Coming!" She announced with a British accent.

I imagined the girl as if she were to wear Goth clothing and her eyes white without pupils or an iris in them. I even wondered if she was going to act like she had been cursed or wicked. I stepped back, ready to see if she was like how I imagined. When Aveline opened the door, I was shocked. She was not like anything I imagined her to be at all.

"Hello," she said with that British accent.

"Um, hi, my name is—"

"Oooo! Is your dragon here to be friends with Porcupine?" She interrupted me.

"Uh, actually no, we're not here for—"

"Wait, don't tell me out here. It's kind of chilly. Come inside where it's warm!" She stopped me again.

"Oh, OK," I said.

As Niko and I followed Aveline inside, the mansion looked so much better inside than from the outside and her British accent just made it even better. She led us into what looked like a living room, and we all sat down. Again, she looked far from what I imagined her to be. Instead, she looked like a cute mystery girl. She had on one of those detective hats and it was a light brown, as was the rest of her clothing. She wore a detective coat with three buttons on the front and it seemed like it was bigger than her size. Not to mention she also had brown Lifestride Adley boots with long white socks.

"So," Aveline started, "what were your names again?"

"My name is Wolverine, and this is Niko," I reminded her.

"Wonderful!" She clapped. "Is Niko here for Porcupine?"

"Erm, no, actually …" I stopped. A giant, long, spiky night dragon came into the room with a large book on his head.

"Was this the book you wanted?" The prickly creature asked with a voice that was powerful and deep. Now I knew why Aveline called the dragon, *Porcupine*.

As Aveline answered with a yes, Porcupine traced alongside the room with a stop by me. My eyes were on him too, intensely. He then looked at Niko who was eyeing something else.

"Aveline, we haven't had any guests in a long time, have we?" Porcupine said as he grinned at me.

"Yeah, but I'm so glad we do now, Porcupine!" She said and threw her hands in the air.

"How long has it been since you've had guests?" I asked.

"Oh, for about two years I suppose," Aveline replied sadly.

"Really? But two years isn't that long thou—"

"Actually, Aveline, it was more like three years," Porcupine said quickly, cutting me off in an instant. I gave him a disgusted look.

"Um, are you sure Porcupi—"

"Yep. It was three years," he cut off Aveline also.

"Uh, OK then. Three years I meant!" She agreed as she went back to her usual enthusiastic voice.

"Oh, well, three years is kind of a long time," I said, even though I was pretty sure it was probably two years as Aveline said.

"Anyway, what were you saying about why you guys were here?" Aveline asked me.

Porcupine looked at me very concerningly. I froze. I didn't want to tell Aveline that Porcupine was a monster and for that I would have to kill him in front of her. I didn't know what he would do to me if I said that to her. So, I decided to lie.

But before I could speak, she said, "Wait! Hold that answer. My green tea is ready. Porcupine, would you mind keeping these two company while I tend to the tea?"

Porcupine looked mad. "OK," he murmured.

I was so glad Aveline had asked that. But when I looked at Porcupine, he was annoyed. When Aveline left, I kind of wished she were still here because of Porcupine's attitude. As the door closed behind her, a silent hush took over the room. No one made a peep.

"So," Porcupine asked abruptly. "What is the reason you are here?"

This was when I couldn't lie. I had to tell him. Whether he jump at me or not, I had to tell him. I would slash at him right away if I needed to. I put my hand on my sword just in case.

"I'm here to try to make Aveline hate you and we're going to destroy you, once, and for all." I told him boldly.

Silence again fell over the room. I was worried he might jump at me any second now but instead he let out an enormous laugh. Niko and I just looked at him, disgustedly. Then he began to speak. "Do you think that a weakling like you and your frail-looking buddy could destroy, *me?*" His tone was powerful and king-like.

I looked at him. He looked at me, thinking he had won.

For a moment I wondered. *Could I? Of course, I could. Didn't I just defeat a huge worm? It was much bigger than Porcupine.*

So, I said, "Yes."

He looked at me in a very disbelieving manner. "How so?" He wanted to know.

Then I replied, "Not too long ago I killed my first victim as my mission. It was a giant earthworm that was far more massive than you, I can tell you that."

He stared at me, then at a wall that was on the left side of me for a long time. He looked like he didn't believe me but at the same time, he did. After what felt like an eternity of silence, he finally said, "OK, then." I was shocked that was all he said. To be honest, I expected more.

At that moment, Aveline entered the room. "OK! Where were we?" She asked happily with a huge grin on her face while holding on to her green tea.

"Aveline," Porcupine announced with a smirk directed at me, "our guest has already spoken of it with me while you were gone,"

My heart skipped a beat.

"Really? Well, I can't wait to hear it, Porcupine! So, Wolverine, what is it?" Aveline asked expectantly.

I was so scared that I could hardly breathe, but the part that made me even more afraid was the fact that Porcupine's eyes were so evilly locked onto me. I knew that this time I couldn't lie, and I had to tell her the truth. It was her safety after all. So, I told her, "Aveline, this dragon is too dangerous for you to be with," I told her in a sad tone.

Aveline's face turned pale like she was going to faint. "What, do you mean?" She asked as her voice faded in sadness.

I began to feel sorrowful for her. "What I mean, Aveline, is that this type of dragon is a trickster and a mind-controlling beast. He is using you, Aveline, and you need to know this. It's for your own good!"

She glared at me for a long time. I could see the expression of despair on her face. She really loved this dragon, but I had to let her know that this dragon was taking over her life.

"No," she disagreed. "It can't be. I-I don't believe you! You have no proof! Porcupine is not like that at all!"

It was true. I didn't have proof. How could Aunt Cornelia expect me to come here and convince Aveline without any proof? This was going to tougher than I thought.

How could I make her believe me?

Just then I noticed that Niko's eyes widened as if he remembered something important. "What is it, Niko?"

Niko looked up at Porcupine with a nasty expression and his eyes got even wider as he yelled to Porcupine, "You."

All eyes went on Porcupine who became extremely nervous.

"What about Porcupine?" I questioned Niko.

"I've seen him before," Niko revealed. He growled at the top of his lungs from the realization. "Your name isn't Porcupine. Your name is Nightfang! But that's not all. You killed my brother!"

101

Chapter 9

The Gruesome Demon

Aveline's face began to turn even more pale. Nightfang froze. I was stunned. I didn't know Niko had a brother! Then, Aveline looked at Nightfang and visibly holding back tears asked, "Is this true?"

At first there was silence, then he said, "I don't remember that."

Niko became furious. He was so furious that he leaped toward Nightfang to give him a piece of his mind and before I could tell him no, he was already on top of him, biting his neck. Nightfang was having a troublesome time getting Niko off of him. I was scared Niko might get hurt, so I quickly tried to make him let go of Nightgang. During the chaos, Aveline stood there yelping, "No, my Porcupine, no!"

It wasn't long before Niko stopped quarreling and when he did, he was snarling and growling in his throat while I was breathing heavily.

Aveline didn't know what to do or what to say and neither did Nightfang or Niko. So, I spoke up. "Niko, you shouldn't have done that. There could have been another way to sort it out with words, *not* violence," I said sternly.

"But Nightfang lied to Aveline. He told her he didn't kill *my* brother. Wouldn't you be that way if someone lied to you about killing your brother?" Niko questioned me.

I wouldn't try to kill them like you tried to with Nightfang!" I answered.

As the bickering continued, Nightfang started to giggle and Aveline noticed. She began to believe that what Wolverine said about her pet was true. He was a monster and nothing but evil.

Once the fighting stopped, Niko and I apologize to each other for our actions. Then I started toward Aveline.

"Aveline … look, I'm sorry that I have to make you let go of Nightfang. But—" Someone stopped me.

"I don't think that will ever happen," Nightfang interrupted. He looked profoundly serious.

Aveline spoke up then, stepped up and asked, "And why do you think that way?"

Nightfang had suddenly become confused. Niko and I were confused too.

Wasn't Aveline just on Nightfang's side a minute ago?

"Aveline," Nightfang said sweetly, "what makes you speak to your beloved pet this way?"

"Don't be wily, *Nightfang*, I noticed you while Wolverine and Niko were bickering," said Aveline.

Nightfang became nervous now. "I, what do you mean?" He asked her.

"You're foolish to think that I'm so silly. I finally saw it Nightfang," she said.

I could see fear in his eyes that he really didn't want this to happen. He was looking at me and Aveline back and forth, panicking. Just then he sprang at me, so I used one of Leroy's powers I remembered and *boom*, Nightfang flopped to ground with an enormous thud.

Niko was incredulously stunned. He had not known the extent of my powers. For a while, I had forgotten that I had powers too. I was relieved I had done that just in time. But my adrenaline was on fire after what just happened.

Nightfang was really mad now. I could see the fire in his eyes. He was breathing intensely, and when he looked at me it was like I was seeing my worst nightmare. His claws were so hard on the ground that it looked like they would crumble into pieces. Everyone just stood there, watching him.

"You," Nightfang said. "You fool! You turned me down the first time, but I will never give up. I am more powerful than you and I will prove it to you. You cannot defeat me. You beings are no match for me. Not even that pesky dragon you have can defeat me. Who do you think you are!" His voice boomed even louder.

I looked at him confidently and replied, "If you say you are more powerful than me, then what causes you to be defeated by just a bit of blazing fire? Look at yourself. You're bent down to your knees, but I am standing tall and bold. Who do you think you are?"

With a snicker that couldn't be seen but could be heard, he said, "You will not be standing for long!" Nightfang lunged out at me again until he almost hit Aveline, when out of nowhere she ran right in front of me.

"Stop!" Aveline shouted.

"Aveline! What are you doing!?" I cried. When Nightfang saw Aveline, he had just barely run into her skirt, coming to a screeching stop on the slippery floor.

Why would Aveline move in front of me like that. She knew she could have been hurt. Doesn't she know better?

"Please!" She begged. "Don't do this!"

I didn't know what Nightfang was thinking. All of a sudden, he pushed her away and growled at her. "Agh!" Aveline was devastated. She thought if Nightfang could see how sad she was about his behavior, it would affect him. But no, she was wrong.

Then Nightfang hissed at Wolverine, "Look at me now, then! I'm not on my knees anymore, am I?"

A shiver of fear went down my spine. Niko was still frozen and Aveline was emotionally and physically hurt.

What could I do now?

But then I realized that I hadn't even tried out any of Ariella's powers yet.

Could one of her powers help me through this situation?

I had to try. So, without any planning, I closed my eyes and all of a sudden, I felt like I was pulled up from the ground, floating in the air. Then, even though my eyes were closed, I saw a white glow all around me and my thoughts were filled with the Holy Spirit and prayers. After that I raised my hands and then the glow sped toward Nightfang at full speed and blasted him. He screeched in anger.

My jaw dropped. An ugly and scary-looking creature out of nowhere came out of Nightfang. The creature looked to be a male spirit. It was almost as tall as Ganon. His arms were so long, and his claws were as big as a grizzly bear. His eyeballs were black, and he had huge goat horns. His skin was dark red.

Aveline was horrified at the fact that the dragon that she had lived with for years had so much evilness inside of him, and she had never noticed it. I felt so bad for her that she had to see it now. Tears started rolling down her cheeks even more. She couldn't believe it and I couldn't believe it either.

"Well," he said in an ugly voice that was painful to hear. "Look, what we have here." He looked around and when his eyes met Aveline's he puffed up. She began to look even more frightened. "Oh, Aveline, why are you so afraid of me? Don't you know who I am? We've known each other for years!"

Aveline took a step back.

"Oh dear! I'm not going to do any harm unto you. I just want to know why you are so afraid of me!" He asked again as he took a step forward.

"Why were *you* inside my friend's soul?" Aveline asked.

He cocked his head slowly and replied, "Why? Because he asked me."

Niko, Aveline, and I were confused. Why would Nightfang want an evil spirit to come inside of him?

"Why would he do that? Why would anyone do such a thing?" Aveline asked, but we all wanted to know.

His eyes penetrated hers as he asked, "Are you sure you want the truth?"

"What truth?" Niko asked suddenly, a little tempered.

He lightly chuckled and said, "Why Niko, you already know the truth. It has just, been a while."

"What happened?" I asked.

He turned around to me quickly and answered, "Well, this was back in the times when Niko and Nightfang were best friends."

"Best ... FRIENDS!?" Niko repeated. "No, I think I wouldn't remember being friends with a dragon named Nightfang."

"That's because it was a long time ago. I already told you that," he said, rolling his eyes.

108

"Who are you anyway?" Niko asked him.

He giggled and replied, "My name is Agwel and I am from Ganon's kingdom."

"Ganon?" Aveline questioned. "You mean, the most powerful demon in the land? I've seen him before. In fact, he has spoken to me before. But it was a long time ago."

"What was it about?" I asked her.

"Well, Ganon told me that—"

"It's actually private. She needs to keep it to herself and herself only," Agwel interrupted.

"OK," I said with a discouraged look on my face.

"Look," Niko started to say, "just tell me how Nightfang and I were friends."

Agwel nodded and said, "Very well then. It's a long story but I'll tell you what happened."

"Good," said Niko.

"Long ago, back when Wolverine was just about one years old, Niko was just a child and lived with his parents and his brother in the big land of Envia. There, he had everything he needed. Lots of rivers, food, shelter, and peace. Lots of other dragons lived there too. So, that's how you met Nightfang. Your brother, Nyka, was jealous of Nightfang because of your close relationship with him. So Nyka tried to kill Nightfang. When Nightfang knew what Nyka was planning, he was scared because he wasn't as powerful as

Nyka. So, he asked in his prayer for a demon to come inside of him so he could be stronger."

"Why did he ask a demon and not an angel?" Niko insisted.

"Because where you used to live, they had tribes of many kinds and all of them had different beliefs. Nightfang's tribe believed that demons were more powerful than angels."

"Oh," Niko said.

"So, when the day came for Nyka to kill Nightfang, he realized that he was extraordinarily strong and Nyka was demented because of it. That's how Nyka died. At the same moment when Nyka was killed, you went to hang out with Nightfang and when you noticed your brother's body, you were devasted to see Nightfang standing there right beside Nyka with blood all over. Nightfang tried to explain it to you, Niko, but you didn't want to listen because all you cared about at that time was your brother. So, you stopped playing with him, you stopped hanging out with him, you stopped speaking to him, and you stopped being best friends with him because of the memories that haunted you of Nyka being killed by Nightfang."

"But … I don't remember all of that happening," Niko said sadly.

"Do you want to know why?" Agwel questioned.

"W-Why?" Niko asked nervously.

With a sigh Agwel answered, "It's because Ganon erased your memory."

"Why would he do that?" Niko question Agwel.

Agwel shrugged and replied, "I don't know. He erases the memories of all the dragons he captures. And to be honest, it looked fairly painful."

As Aveline was listening to the conversation, she noticed that Nightfang was silent and looked weak and sick. "Nightfang? Are you OK?"

Everyone looked over to where Nightfang was. He was in a hunched position and looked uncomfortable. With a faint whisper in his voice he responded, "I think so."

"Well, just so you know, there has been a demon inside of you for many years," Aveline told him.

"But, how?" Nightfang asked in confusion. "Why?"

"I'll tell you why," Niko volunteered. "This demon here named Agwel told me how it got to that point. So, here's why. Nightfang, do you remember Nyka? My brother?"

After a minute of hard thinking, he then answered, "Yes."

"And do you remember that he tried to kill you?"

This time he responded, "No."

"Apparently, Ganon erased your memory too, but we don't know why. Do you remember me?" Niko pushed.

Nightfang looked at Niko for a long time. "Actually, I think I do."

"We were best friends, remember?" Niko said, with almost a happy expression on his face. Slowly, he was beginning to remember too.

"Yeah," Nightfang said, as memories began to resurface.

I had goosebumps from watching this. I was happy but sad at the same time. Agwel was annoyed by it and had a frown on his face as if he were having a bad day.

I still wondered why demons always had to look that way.

Once everything was settled, Agwel said, "I think I should be going so that my master won't get mad at me for not returning to his kingdom."

"Wait!" I said to Agwel.

"What is it now?" Agwel seem annoyed.

"Do you have at least a small clue as to why your master erases the memories of dragons?" I asked.

With a loud sigh, he said, "Maybe. But I can't tell you anyway. Ganon will be mad."

"OK," I said with a frustrated look.

When Agwel left, Aveline came over to me with a cheerful look and said, "Wolverine, thank you for being here to help my friend. I didn't know there was something wrong with him and I'm sorry I got a little worked up in the beginning."

"It's alright," I said with understanding. "Of course, you didn't realize it. That's why I had to come here."

She nodded and asked, "Who knew and told you that Nightfang was cursed?"

"It was an old lady name Aunt Cornelia. She lives not too far from where I live, a placed called The Two Kingdoms. She also lives in a home where there are many potions and spell books and all of them were gifted to her from the fairies," I told her.

"The fairies? You mean, the ones that live on the other side of the Dark Woods?" Aveline asked.

"Yes," I replied. "But about Aunt Cornelia, I'm not really sure who she is."

Aveline shrugged and said, "Maybe you'll know one day."

"Yeah," I hopefully agreed, "maybe one day.

Chapter 10

My Second Encounter

A crow awoke me, and I was bewildered as to where I was. I found myself lying on a hard, wooden plank in an old small, wooden hut. The air smelled dry, and the cold wind made me shake. As I got to my feet, I went to look around but sadly, there was nothing here but the wooden plank. There weren't even any windows, only a door.

I went outside to see where I was and unfortunately it was a place that I'd been before. It looked like the place where Oleana and her people lived, and it was. Since it was dark out, I thought the people would be sleeping right now but it turned out no one was in their houses. Which was strange. I decided to look for them.

As I was walking around, I saw people behind a house that was much bigger than the other houses, which, I'm guessing meant it would be Oleana's. But I also noticed someone else there. I squinched my eyes closer to see who it was. Sure enough, it was Ganon.

Why?

I stayed put to hear their conversation.

"Oleana, do you know why I am here?" He asked with an angry look on his face as he crossed his arms.

"Yes, sir," she replied as she looked down.

"I thought we were keeping it a secret!" Ganon growled. "Why did you tell her?!"

"I'm sorry, sir, it won't happen again. Please give me another chance," she begged.

Ganon looked at her for a long time with a displeased look and said, "I don't give people who work for me chances, lady. You've upset me badly once and I can't let that happen again. You're wasting my time! Do you not understand?" He shouted.

"I understand, sir," she responded softly.

"Hmph ... seems to me that you don't!" He replied sternly.

As I was watching the conversation, someone noticed me and yelled, "Someone else is here! They're spying!"

"Oh no!" I thought. *What was I going to do now? Someone had already spotted me. Should I hide?*

I couldn't. There wasn't a good hiding spot around. By the look of my surroundings, there was nowhere here to hide.

So, I decided to go up to them instead.

"Ganon, why are you being so rude to her?" I asked him.

When he faced me, he grinned the same evil grin I had grown to hate. It was creepy.

Instead of him answering my question, he said, "Ah, Wolverine! It's so nice to see you again," though, deep down I suspected he was still upset from our last encounter.

"I don't think so," I said. "Because I think that from now on it'll be bad news every time I'll have to see you again."

He frowned at that response. Then Oleana said, "Wolverine? What in the world are you doing here? This isn't safe! You need to leave!"

"Oleana, I wanted her to be here. It was my calling for her to be here," said Ganon.

I was puzzled.

What did this fool want now?

As Ganon walked up to me, Oleana warned, "Don't hurt her!"

Ganon stopped, chuckled, and said, "I would never do that now, would I?"

Liar. I said to myself,

He probably hurt Niko a while back too.

"A monster like you would!" Oleana said again but this time louder.

His look when she said that was irate. He turned to Oleana and glared at her for a long time. Oleana stood frozen, wishing she hadn't said that to him. Then Ganon smiled again and said, "You know, I never realized you could be so stubborn. Of all the stubborn people, I think you are the most stubborn person I've ever met."

Oleana's jaw dropped, and she shouted, "HOW DARE YOU CALL ME STUBBORN, YOU MONSTER. I WILL—"

"You will what?" He asked severely.

Oleana stood frozen again. Then Ganon squinched his eyes and said, "That's what I thought," then turned back to me, simpering.

As he walked up to me, I was getting more and more nervous. But I kept my chin high at all times and maintained my cool. I thought if I retained that demeanor with him, he wouldn't dare talk to me like he was talking to Oleana.

When he stopped walking, he quickly made his face serious and asked, "Where is it?"

I was demented. *What was he talking about?*

"Where is what?" I asked back.

He stamped his foot at me and said, "Give it to me now, you idiot! I don't have time for your silly games! Pass it on!"

The movement he made was so unexpected that I jumped. I didn't know what to tell him. When I thought harder about what he wanted, I remembered. It was the white gem that Niko was telling me about! Niko said Ganon thought that I had it!

"Oh? You mean the silver gem? I'm sorry, but I don't have it," I told him as I tried to get back into my solid position with my chin held high.

Ganon gave a slight growl and said, "I'm sure you met one of my helpers named Agwel, right? He's been helping me with my beautiful plan, and he told me that one day recently he saw you with it on you. Now," he said as he walked closer to me, "of all things, I wouldn't think he would just lie to me like that. He's one of the best. So … stop joking with me and hand it over before there's trouble involved."

"I'm telling you the truth, Ganon. Like I said, I don't have it."

He looked at me for so long. I wondered how he was not blinking. Then he finally said, "OK, then," and walked away.

Was that all? I wondered.

It was reassuring that was all he wanted to talk to me about, so I breathed out deeply, feeling relieved. Then, right after I took a breath, Ganon suddenly took a swing at me. I wasn't prepared, so I got hit, bad. It was very painful. I fell to the ground.

"NO," Oleana screamed. "You liar! Why would you do that?! Leave her alone. You know she's just a young girl!"

Ganon rolled his eyes and agreed, "Hmm … probably only fifteen or sixteen."

"Fourteen," I corrected, wiping my mouth which was covered in blood.

"See! She's too young! You can't do that!" Oleana admonished him.

Ganon ignored her and said to Wolverine, "So, you're saying that Agwel is just lying to me? Huh? Are you?!"

While Ganon was yelling at me, all I could feel was pain. There was pain in my arms, legs, and feet. I was so scared that tears ran down my cheeks. Ganon noticed how scared I was and he made fun of me. "Look at you now, Wolverine. You've told me before that you were more powerful than me. But look what's happening now. Look! You're scared and crying!" He laughed hard.

I wanted to cry even more, but I kept it in. I thought about how Madeline and Victoria would be if they saw this happening. I knew they would stick up for me even though they knew it wasn't enough. I wished they were here right now, badly. I got up on my feet while my legs wobbled trying to balance my body, looked at him in the eyes, and told him as boldly as possible, "I … *am not* … *scared.* Think about that twice!"

He looked down at me, still grinning. This time I saw a little bit of his teeth showing. I tried so hard to not show him how scared to death I was. He then made a "hmph" sound and walked away toward Oleana. That was terrifying.

Oleana was exasperated but also petrified when Ganon was walking toward her. She kept stumbling with her words as she was begging. "Please, sir, please! Just give me one more chance!" She said trembling.

"Why would I? You've let me down," he said.

"I know, sir. But please, I'm begging you, I won't let you down again I promise! Please, my people! They are suffering, *please*!" She was starting to burst into tears.

"FINE! But this is the last time. Got it!" He warned with annoyance, as he was looking at her people.

With her mouth hung open, she said, "Oh sir, I won't let you down!"

"You probably will," he angrily muttered. "Goodbye!"

"Wait!" I shouted after him.

Ganon turned to me and said, "What?!"

I stood still for a split second and said, "I need to ask you this one thing."

He let out a long sigh and growled, "I don't have time for your silly questions, so make it quick!"

"OK, well, I'm just wondering. What made you hate me so much? Why do you want to destroy me? What happened in the past? Why do my parents want me to defeat you? Huh? What happened!?" I was starting to burst into tears again. "If I knew what happened, I would try to sort it out. There has to be an explanation!"

Ganon froze. "I'm afraid I cannot answer that question," he said with a low, sad tone.

"C-Can you at least give me a clue?" I pressed him.

He looked at me even more glum and answered, "It's about you and my brother. Now goodbye."

"Huh? What about—" It was too late. He had disappeared.

I woke up seeing the sun beaming warmth upon my face and I could hear the birds singing songs. From underneath I could feel the prickly grass tickling me. As I got up, I remembered the face Ganon made and for some reason I wondered why. I decided to tell Niko about it. Afterall, it was especially important.

When I went to find Niko, I found him lying on his back, his eyes resting. I went to get his attention. "Hey, Niko?"

Niko quickly started his eyes on me and responded, "Yes?"

"I've had another dream about Ganon," I told him.

Niko was suddenly shocked. "Again?"

"Yes, again! But it was also like a message as with the last one. The only difference was that there were different situations that happened in both of the dreams that I had."

"OK, so, what happened in this dream?" He asked.

"Remember that place we went to where we had to fight that worm?" I asked.

"Yes. You mean that place where our first mission was? Where Oleana and her people lived?" Niko recalled.

"Yes, exactly!" I replied. "But also, Ganon was there too. You see, I woke up in one of the little houses and tried to figure out where I was, and unfortunately, I noticed that I was in the area where Oleana and her people lived. After that I looked around until I heard a familiar voice, which was Oleana's. The voice was heard from behind her house, so I went to see who she was talking to. There, I saw Ganon. I noticed that while I was spying on them, Ganon was angry because Oleana told me the secret that she and Ganon meant to keep between them."

"Man," said Niko.

"I know. She kept begging Ganon to give her another chance, until one of her people saw me watching them. That's when the chaos started happening. When Ganon saw that I was there, he grinned like it was all part of his plan for me to be present. Which, I was. While Ganon and I were talking, he started walking toward me like he was about to do something and Oleana started shouting at him to not hurt me. He said he wouldn't, but he lied and after that he hit me."

"What were you and Ganon talking about?" Niko asked.

"That silver gem you were talking to me about. You were right. He actually thought that I had it. I kept telling him that I didn't have it, but he just wouldn't trust me. So that's why he hit me. He said that Agwel said that I had it on me. But as Ganon was leaving I stopped him."

"For what?" Niko questioned.

I-I had this question I kept in for a long time. Way back from when my parents told me I had to fight Ganon. I asked him why he hated me so much and why did I have to destroy him," I told Niko.

"I bet he didn't even answer, did he?" Niko asked.

"Actually, he did. Even though he only answered me with a hint. He told me that it was about me and his brother. But I don't understand the hint he shared with me. Do you think you know, Niko?" I asked him.

"No," he replied in a low tone. "No, I don't."

"Well … maybe it doesn't matter right now at this point. C'mon, Niko, let's go," I ordered.

Ten minutes passed as we were flying. When I looked at my tracker, it told us that we only had three more destinations to go until we arrived at Ganon's kingdom. I was so thrilled because I really wanted to get this journey over with. As I looked on the other side of my screen to see which destination I would have to go next, it told me that we were headed to a little town named Orker Village. It was bigger than the town Oleana and her people lived in. Much, much bigger.

"My tracker is saying that we are going to another town and on my screen, it looks way bigger than Oleana's. It's called Orker Village," I told Niko.

"Alright!" He responded.

Five minutes passed and something in the distance alerted us from far away. It looked like a storm, and it was a massive one. "Wolverine, this isn't looking too good. Huge thunderclouds are heading right for us," Niko warned.

"Darn it," I replied in frustration. "Do think we could go around it somehow?"

"With this one, I don't think we will be able to," he replied.

I sighed and said, "I guess we will have to fly through it then."

We were then awfully close to the storm and lightning flashed and thunder boomed loudly. Rain poured down as we tried to get through the dark, thick, heavy clouds. My body, clothes, and hair were so damp and cold. I tried to hold on to Niko as tightly as I could for warmth but since I was so damp, it didn't help at all. I was shivering and couldn't keep my teeth from chattering. I didn't know how Niko was seeing anything.

Finally, we were almost out of the thunderstorm and Niko and I were wetter than ever. As we neared the end, the wind and the rain became even colder. I continued to hold on to Niko as tight as I could, but I felt myself slipping off his scales. It seemed like every time I tried to grip tighter, I just kept slipping. I started panicking inside but tried to keep my cool on the outside.

With all his might, Niko was trying to overcome the wind and the rain. The wind made it so hard for him to push through, while the rain made it hard for him to see anything in front of him. We both really didn't know how far we were from the end. But we just hoped that it would all come to pass soon. I really hoped so.

At last, we made it through before I was sure I would fall off Niko. I was so glad we made it out of that storm. Both of us were dripping with so much rain and I was shivering uncontrollably now. But we were all right. I prayed we wouldn't get sick behind this. That wouldn't be great.

Ten minutes passed and while we were soaring, Niko was the first to discover our destination. "We're here!" He announced.

"Hallelujah," I shouted joyfully, still trembling.

We landed in the middle of Orker Village. When people noticed us landing, at first, they were scared but when they saw how damp and cold we were, they immediately invited us into their shops and homes to warm us up. We were so thankful. They took us into a warm, cozy building with a fireplace inside. They moved a chair closer to the fireplace for me so I could feel the warmth better while they let Niko rest near it on a big blanket spread out.

While I was settling in, they brought me some chamomile tea and a big rectangular container with warm water to unthaw my legs and feet. The people, and the place that I was in, were all that I needed at this point. Then a person who was a female came into the room to ask questions.

"Hello," she said in a low voice, "my name is Johanna and I have a question that I want to ask you."

"What is it?" I asked.

"Some of the people here and I were wondering why you are here," she asked.

"My name is Wolverine, and this is Niko," I responded. "We have come here from The Two Kingdoms to help you

126

and the others. We have helped a lot of people like you. You see, our goal is to reach Ganon and to slay him once and for all. Do you know who Ganon is?"

"Oh yes, I've heard of you before and I have also heard of Ganon as well. We people of the Orker Village thinks he's nice. Why do you want to destroy him?" Johanna asked.

I was stunned.

Nice?

Ever since I'd heard about him, and every time I spoked to him, he was never a "nice" person. Well, except when he answered my question about why he hated me so much. His tone was glum when he said it was about me and his brother. I still wanted to know what happened.

"Nice?" I repeated with a surprised tone.

"Of course. He always gave us the resources we needed for our town. We used to have little. But thanks to him, we have more than we need," she replied.

"Everything?"

"Everything," she replied.

"Well, that's a little strange," I said.

"Why do you say that?" Johanna asked confused.

"While I was on my journey, there was this town I arrived at and this lady named Oleana, the leader, was telling me everything about how Ganon gave them so little of everything and was just very cruel to them," I explained.

127

Johanna didn't say anything for a short while. She then said, "Oh, well, that's concerning. Do you know why?"

"I can't really put a finger on it," I said.

Again, she was silent for a time before she nodded and added, "I'm going to head out." She got up quickly like she was in a hurry and shut the door hard with a bang.

As the door closed, I started to wonder why Ganon was treating Oleana and her people unfairly but treating the town of this village fairly. It was all very strange to me.

Did Oleana do something that Ganon didn't like? That had to be it. But what could she have done? Maybe she stole something from Ganon that was important.

Five minutes passed and the door clicked open to reveal a man. The door closed hard behind him as I studied him. He looked serious and disappointed as he approached me. Was Johanna talking to him about what I just said. If so, he looked like he was a little unhappy with what I said about Ganon.

"Hello, Wolverine, my name is Leon. Johanna told me about you, and she said that you made her upset with your desire to kill Ganon," he blurted out.

"I did?" I questioned.

"That's what she told me. She is upset about this because we know that if he was killed, he wouldn't be able to give us the resources we need. If that happens, our town will have little, just like from a long time ago. He seems to us like a nice person, or rather half person, half monster I

128

guess, but we need him so our town can be happy. I am the leader of this town. I am the main one who keeps this town organized around here. If any of my people think something's wrong regarding what they see or what they've heard from a traveler whom they think is suspicious, I have to believe them. So, from Johanna's impressions of you and what she heard, I know you are not some regular traveler. You have come here to spread lies to us, haven't you?" He asked me angrily.

"I, n-no. I came here to help you with the problem you have, not to spread lies. I've met Ganon before. Two times he was in my dreams and in both of those dreams, he was shown to be a bad omen every time he showed up. I don't spread false lies to anyone for no apparent reason," I explained.

Leon sighed hard, apparently thinking what to say next. "Alright," he said suddenly. "I'll believe you. Only because I have no other option. But I can't just allow you to help us without my people's acceptance. Stay here."

When Leon left, I patiently waited for him to come back. While I was waiting, I wondered what type of problem this town could have. Everyone here seemed jolly, laughing, and having a great time. But I did notice that at the endpoint of the town, way back, was a very creepy swamp.

Was that the problem Leon was talking about? It could be.

As the door reopened, Leon came to me and said, "OK, my people have accepted your offer to help us. So, I'll tell you about our problem. Did you notice that swamp out at the far end of town?"

"I certainly did," I answered truthfully.

"We call that swamp the Haunted Swamp. It's full of ugly creatures and they're strong. A long time ago, before we ever knew about Ganon, those monsters decided to invade our homes and shops. After the invasion, we had barely any food or supplies. They took most of the food, and almost all of the supplies were broken and destroyed. No one was hurt or anything."

"That's a good thing," I said.

"Yes, it is. But we didn't really have anything during that time and as a leader, it was frustrating for me. For a week we were starving and sick. Then, we saw a huge, tall-looking figure coming through the front entrance. The only thing we saw were red eyes," he described.

"That sounds terrifying."

"It was. But he wasn't the only one who was there. He was holding something that had amber eyes. As he came clear out of the shadows, he looked very frightening as he was holding a long snake around his neck. He scared everyone in the town, including me. We thought he was going to curse us," Leon confessed.

"So, before Ganon came, was the town homeless? You know, you had things that you needed but it wasn't a whole lot?" I questioned.

"Yes. When the monsters came, they took most of what we thought they would take and left us with no medical kits and only a few things to eat," he answered.

"I see," I replied.

"Yes, anyway, Ganon was very scary when we first encountered him. When he spoke, he said he was going to help us. We didn't know how he knew about the chaos, but I thought if we didn't get help soon, we would be in poverty and I didn't want my town to suffer any longer, so I let him. To be honest with you, it was the best decision I ever made, and my people now are well and happy. So, I'm not sure why you would want to defeat Ganon. He has helped us with so much of what we needed."

"Ganon has been known to do some evil things. He does not like me and although I was trained to stop him, I can't help but think his feelings about me are deeper than that. I believe it has something to do with my parents and why they sent me away only to bring me back. I once asked Ganon about it and all he confirmed was that it was about me and his brother. I still don't quite understand. I want to ask you something. Do you know who Ganon's brother is or what his name is?" I questioned Leon.

"A while ago I read some things about him and the only thing that I remember seeing was that his name was Gydon and that he has a rare symbol on his back. Of everyone I know, no one truly knows what it means. But anyway, let me take you to the swamp," Leon said changing the subject.

"Alright," I said.

As we walked toward the Haunted Swamp, I noticed that it was getting darker. When we came to a stopping point, Leon said, "Well, this is it," and left.

Niko and I looked at each other, wondering if we should take a step closer. But as we tried to see under the swamp, a weird-looking monster jumped out at us as quickly as an alligator. "Stay back!" Niko shouted to the creature as it almost got me. That was a close call.

Instead of my sword, I got out the axe and quickly hit the monster hard in its stomach. It yelled in pain and anger. The monster looked like a gargoyle but with no wings. It was so ugly, and it barely had any fleshy skin, it was mostly bone. The monster's movements were also really weird.

"Aaarrgghh!" It growled loudly.

"Niko! What is it doing!?" I asked. But before Niko could respond, more of the ugly creatures came out from underneath the swamp and started growling at us in anger. All of them looked like the one that scared us.

I knew I had to stand my ground. There were six of them in total. "Niko, fight the three over there and I'll fight the three over here. Got it?"

"Got it," he nodded.

As he went for the other three, I gripped my axe and hit the same one, this time in the head. It fell to the ground with a thud. Then one of them tried to quickly lunge at my neck so

I spun out of the way and stabbed him in the back. Then the other one sneakily grabbed my neck again from behind, so I butted my head back as hard as I could, knocking him out. He too fell to the ground with a thud. After that I stomped on his head and a gruesome sound was made.

When I was done, I took huge, deep breaths and made my way toward Niko to help him out. He only had one opponent left who appeared weak, so I let Niko take it down.

When the fight was over, we heard a rumbling sound beneath the swamp. As it came out into sight, it looked like the ones we fought but was bigger, and it looked stronger too. It was time to get back to business.

"Argghh!" It roared. "You have defeated those pesky monsters that have tried to defeat you. But you will never be able to destroy, *me!*"

"Try us!" I responded back.

He growled in anger again and lunged forward at us. I gripped onto my axe again and lunged at him as well. I tried to stab him in the side but instead he grabbed my weapon and turned it over so hard, it turned me around too and hit me on my back. As I fell, he was about to stomp on my head until Niko leaped toward him and made him fall to the ground. Niko then instantly bit down on the monster's left shoulder.

The monster yelled and then furiously punched Niko in the eye. Niko, whining in pain, rolled over to the left side of the creature. It then got up quickly and took a long swing at me, but I grabbed its wrist and quickly twisted it 360 degrees and punched him right in the chin, and his head flung straight up so I pushed him hard down to the ground. Then, I stomped on his head and after that, I was certain he was dead.

After all that I said to Niko, "That was rough, wasn't it?"

"Definitely," he replied. "Though this was the toughest battle we've ever faced and it's only the second time we have done so. I think we should head back."

"You're right. Let's go."

As we arrived back at the town, we saw Leon lying down beside a shop, waiting. We both quickly walked toward him so he wouldn't have to wait any longer. As we went up to him, he immediately stood up and turned toward us. "Did you destroy all of them?" He asked in an ecstatic way.

"Sure did," I answered.

Leon's eyes opened wide with a surprised look on his face. "Really? All of them? Even that huge one?"

"Yes, all of them. It was pretty scary because I almost got crushed by one of those things. But Niko managed to push him out of the way just in time. So yes, we slayed each and every one that was there," I said proudly.

"Well, well that's great! Now we don't have to worry about if they ever invade our town again! Anyway, I was wondering if you would like to stay here for the night since you're going somewhere that is really far away. We do have a hotel here," he told us.

"Of course. Thanks!" I said.

"Good! I'll show you your room that you will be staying in for the night," Leon offered.

As we were about to move, I stopped him and asked, "What about Niko? Where will he sleep?"

"He can sleep outside," he replied.

"OK, that's fine," I said.

When we arrived at the hotel, I dropped Niko off at the front of the building and followed Leon inside. He led me to a room and asked me if I had any questions. When I told him no, he left and went on his way.

I flopped on my bed to calm down from the things I had done so far. I realized that I'd done so many things during my journey. Now there were only two more worlds ahead before I would arrive at Ganon's kingdom. I hoped things on my next mission wouldn't be as involved as the others.

As I thought about what I needed to do, I also thought about taking a warm shower. I had done so much these past couple of days. So that's what I did.

Later, sitting in bed, I stared out the window and saw that it was turning dark. I decided to sleep so I could get some rest. I made my way under the covers and stared up at the ceiling, trying to think of anything other than the confusing confession of Ganon about his brother.

Successfully, I quieted those thoughts and immediately fell into a deep slumber.

Chapter 11

The Promise

I awoke from sleep feeling drowsy but also ready to start a new and adventurous day. There was a clock on a nightstand beside me with the time. It was a quarter to eight. I looked out the window to see what the people were doing at this time of day. Some of them were opening up their shops and going to work or taking their children to school, while others were just enjoying the early morning breeze.

I went to wash up and dress before going down to breakfast. When I was all done, I walked down to the main lobby to fill up my stomach. Thirty minutes later I was finished, so I went out through the door to get to Niko. His eyes started to open as I was walking toward him. "Good morning, Niko!" I greeted him.

When he saw me, he responded, tiredly, "Good morning."

"Ready to start another adventurous day?"

Niko immediately smiled and replied, "Always."

"Then let's go tell Leon that we're leaving. But before we do, let me feed you your breakfast," I said.

"No need," he said.

"How come?" I asked.

"Some kids fed me a while ago. I'm still a little full so I think we can go let Leon know that we're leaving."

"Oh, OK. Let's go then," I agreed.

"Wait, before we take a step, I need to stretch."

I crossed my arms, rolled my eyes, and said, "Fine, I'll let you do your business."

After that we went to Leon who was finishing up a conversation. When we arrived, he ended it, noticed us and turned towards us.

"Thank you for letting me help with the problem that you had and for giving me a room at the hotel," I said.

"No problem, and I am glad that I accepted your help," Leon admitted. "Goodbye!"

I smiled and waved.

"Ready?" Niko asked, waiting for me to get on his back.

As I got on his back, I answered, "Ready when you are!"

Niko spread his wings and took off in a flash. I was so glad that we only had two more worlds to go to before we reached Ganon's kingdom. It was going to be an achievement for both of us. Something we would never forget. Including the first time we met and started to have a friendship.

When we were above the clouds now, I looked at my tracker to see the next destination that we had to go to. I was more than a little surprised. There was a question mark before the word *kingdom*. I then saw a map icon that showed how much I'd done and how much more I needed to do before I got to Ganon. When I clicked on it, it showed a full map of every world I'd been to, except the last two worlds. Mainly the one with the question mark.

"Huh? I exclaimed out loud. "What's with the question mark?"

"What's the problem, Wolverine?" Niko asked.

"This world that we're going to is a kingdom, but there is a question mark in the space where the name should be. I don't understand," I replied.

"That's ... odd," he said concerningly.

"And strange," I added.

"Let's just see what this is all about when we get there. I'm fairly sure we'll know if it's the right location," Niko assured me.

"OK."

The flight almost took forty minutes, but we were able to get there. As we went under the clouds to see if we would be able to spot it, in the distance we both thought that it wasn't the right place because it was enormously big. It wasn't as big as The Two Kingdoms though. Even though we doubted it was the right one, we landed there anyway. The walls inside and out had a mystical grayish-blue tint and had a giant gate made out of hard metal. Two guards were guarding it.

When we finally landed, the guards didn't see us at first but as we walked up to the gate even closer, they spotted us. "Hey, you! You're not allowed to enter this kingdom. Walk along now," said the guard to the left.

"I'm sorry, but you must be mistaken. We've come here for an important reason," I said.

"And what is that?" The guard on the right asked.

"Uh, well you see, I'm on a journey to—"

"I'm sorry, ma'am, but we just can't let you in anyway because our king says to not let anyone in at this hour except for someone he's waiting for." The same guard stopped me.

"Someone he's waiting for? I'm quite sure that's me he's talking about," I reassured the guard.

As the guard on the left was eyeing Niko up and down, he said, "He didn't say the person was going to bring a dragon with them."

"Well, maybe he had forgotten—"

"He always remembers what to tell us and how we will recognize someone he wants to invite into his kingdom," the guard on the right told me.

"Well maybe he didn't this time."

"Well, I think, young lady, you need to leave because our job as guards is to follow our king's word. So, if he says that he did not call for someone to arrive here with a dragon, you are not invited into this kingdom!" The same guard said to me with finality.

"But—"

"Thallus, what is going on?" Asked a very tall and bold human-like creature who looked similar to Ganon. When he noticed me, he said, "Oh, Wolverine, you're here. Come inside."

Niko and I smirked as we shrugged and walked inside behind him. Then Thallus said, "Wait, My King, you said to not invite … well, you said—"

"Did I not tell the both of you that someone was going to come here with a dragon?"

"Um, n-no?" Thallus replied nodding his head vigorously from side to side. Even the other guard did the same thing.

"Oh, well, I guess I had forgotten to tell you about that. Sorry to the both of you," the king said absently as he left. Right about the time when Thallus was about to say, "it's fine," the gate had already shut.

As Niko and I followed the king inside his massive kingdom, he led us around a corner and then opened a door. When it opened, my eyes widened over just how giant the room was. There were many books neatly and perfectly placed inside each shelf. Niko was amazed, too.

"Wolverine, we will be discussing some things in this library that you really need to know," the king said as he sat at a long table.

"Is there a problem that you have that I need to fix?" I asked him.

"No. The reason why I called you here is because I want you to know something important before you reach Ganon. I … I have a lot to tell." He sighed. "Do you think you can keep up with it?"

"I'll try," I answered.

"This is going to be really direct but, I am Ganon's brother."

I didn't say anything for a long time as I froze. I knew he looked like Ganon but, I didn't think he would be Ganon's brother! "Gydon?"

"Yes, my name is Gydon. But there's more to the story than this," he reported.

"Is it because of the relationship with you and Ganon?" I guessed.

"Yes. In the past, Ganon hated me so much. I tried to help him with all that I could but everything I did never worked out. He said that I was annoying and that I was doing everything wrong for him. You know, I tried my best to help him as a brother, like any brother would do. But he was just so hardheaded and would never use his head. He would never think about all the people he had hurt, especially me."

"Has this always been happening?" I questioned.

"Ever since," he confirmed.

"That must've been awful."

"It was. And then one day, he left and started ruling his own kingdom, while I ruled mine. I sometimes think about him here and there until I get to the point where I miss him. Even though he treated me like I was nothing. But I did see that recently you asked him about why he hated you so much and he implied it was because of you and me."

"Yeah, and I didn't understand how or why. He just left me with no explanation. Are you going to tell me why?"

"Yes. First, I will tell you how. Did you notice a weird symbol on my back?" Gydon asked.

"Yes," I answered.

"You also have it too, and it's also on your back."

"Really? I never realized there was ever anything on my back. Since that's the how, what's the why?" I asked him.

"The reason why my brother has involved you is because since we have the same symbol and since he never liked me, when he sees or thinks of you, it reminds him of me. That's why he wants to get rid of you. He just doesn't want to remember me because it makes him mad," he explained.

"That's … why?" I asked with great surprise.

"That's why," he repeated.

"Wow. Usually, brothers become like best friends. But not you two."

"Yeah. It's hard. But I'm starting to not think about it too much anymore."

"So, is that all you need to tell me?" I asked.

"Not quite. I have one more thing. Do you remember Atlas?"

"Yes," I answered. "I've met him twice before. Does he have anything to do with Ganon?"

"Yes. Eight years ago," Gydon began. Then he opened up his hands and blue magic began to form. Niko and I were amazed. I watched closely as Gydon raised his hands toward the sky and as he let go, a screen appeared before us. As he told the story, the images moved. "Ganon assassinated Atlas because he was a spy who pretended to be a worker for Ganon. He would spy so he could tell Amorok and Alice what he was doing." The images showed Ganon looking at Atlas suspiciously. "Ganon thought he was suspicious, so he followed him to The Two Kingdoms and saw that Atlas was fake. So, one day, when Atlas wasn't looking, Ganon killed him from behind."

"Hold up. Atlas … is… a ghost?" I questioned Gydon.

"That's odd," Niko started. "He looked very much alive when we met him."

"Yes, I know, but he has been gone for a long time," Gydon said.

"How did you know that Atlas was killed on that day?" Niko asked him.

After a long pause, Gydon replied, "On that very same day and at the same time of Atlas's death, I decided that was the day that I would visit my brother. I knew he missed me, and I surely missed him. Even after all of the hard times, I just wanted him to see my face and to see his reaction. I hoped it would be a positive one. But I arrived just in time to see him kill Atlas and I immediately turned away. That is when I knew that Ganon would never change."

Niko yawned, and he decided to rest near a bookcase and lie down.

"Are you ever going to visit him?" I asked.

"Maybe … maybe not," Gydon answered back.

"OK, well, I have one more question to ask you before we leave," I told him.

"Let's hear it."

"Do you know why Ganon hates you? I mean, this whole issue had to come from somewhere," I said.

"Yes, I understand your question, Wolverine, but the thing is, I just don't know. I have been asking myself that same question, but I just can't figure out why he hates me in the first place. It sometimes frustrates me."

"I get it."

As Niko stretched, he accidently knocked several books off the shelf, and they slammed right on top of his head. "Ouch," he yelped loudly.

"Niko!" I called to him in concern.

"No need to worry, young one. I got it," said Gydon. While Gydon was still in his seat, his hands spread open wide toward the books that were on Niko's head and he levitated them back to their proper places.

"Woah, that was amazing! Do you think you will be able to teach me some of that stuff?" I asked him.

"Maybe," he replied.

"Thanks. Anyway, we will be going now," I said.

"Alright," Gydon sighed.

As I was about to open the door, Gydon stopped me and said, "Wait! One more thing before you leave."

"Yes?" I turned.

"Just … just don't kill him. I've decided I do want to see my brother again. Instead of killing him, please change his heart. He needs to understand that this is not the right path to be on. He needs a chance. Do you promise?" He implored.

I thought and thought and finally, I agreed, "Alright, I promise."

Then we left.

Chapter 12

The Talk

When I left Gydon's kingdom, I noticed Thallus staring at me. I didn't see where the other guard was so he must have been on a break. "What do you want?" I asked him.

He shrugged and said, "Nothing. I'm just sorry that I treated you horribly, that's all."

"Well, Thallus, I accept your apology," I said. Thallus nodded at my acceptance.

Then, Niko and I flew up into the air and headed toward our last destination. As we were flying in the air, I checked in with my tracker to see where we were headed next, and it told me that we were to arrive at a home with an old man living inside. I wondered why our last location would be an old man's house before getting to Ganon's kingdom.

Maybe I shouldn't judge. He could be useful in some sort of way.

It wasn't long before we saw the old man's house and you could see that his house was much bigger than Aunt Cornelia's. There were lots of beautiful flowers growing around his house and the grass was so green and cut neat.

As we were about to land, a person came bursting out of the house, waving his arms frantically with a big smile on his face. When we landed, he greeted us. We shook hands and his grip was firm. When he went to greet Niko, he rubbed his head very gently.

"Wolverine! It's so nice to see you again! It's been years since I last saw your face," he said, his voice sounding old and bold.

I looked at him confused.

"Oh, pardon me, I should've known you wouldn't remember. You were a baby when I first saw you. But you're all grown up now and ready to fight Ganon!"

"Urm, yeah," I said nervously, thinking about the promise I made with Gydon.

"Come on, come on! My house is cozy so you can relieve all your worries here," he told me.

"OK," I replied.

As Niko and I followed the old man into his house, a scent of strong cinnamon penetrated throughout the room. He was right, this place was extremely pleasant for someone to rest their thoughts. There were so many potions carefully stacked on the shelf with spell books lined up neatly and a little fireplace in the back. Looking at this home reminded me of Aunt Cornelia's. I remembered she had a fireplace, and her potions and spell books were arranged neatly alongside the walls of her home too.

As I sat down, he offered me lavender tea and I accepted. While he went into another room, I sat down in a chair with Niko perched beside me. It wasn't long before the old man made his way back to the main room and he handed me the beverage. As he sat down across from me, he thought to formally introduce himself.

"Hello, Wolverine, I know you do not remember who I am since it's been forever. But my name is Alatar. Your mother and your father have told me that you are to defeat Ganon, so I just wanted to cheer you on."

"T-Thanks," I said nervously.

Alatar noticed my nervousness.

"Wolverine, are you alright? If something's on your mind, you can tell me," he urged.

"It's just that," I began, "when I went to Ganon's brother, Gydon, he asked me not kill Ganon because that was his brother, and he wants to give him another chance. I felt so sorry for him, I agreed not to kill him. Alatar, I'm not going to kill Ganon."

I was waiting for him to get mad at me but instead he told me in a calm, composed tone, "Yes, changing someone's heart is a better choice. But I just feel like once you go back to The Two Kingdoms and tell them you haven't killed Ganon, Amorok will be very displeased. He is a demon after all, and demons can lose their temper very easily," Alatar explained.

"I guess. When he explained everything to me back at The Two Kingdoms," I said to Alatar, "he sounded very serious, like it was now or never."

"Yes," Alatar agreed. "That is just how demons are made to be."

"I have a question. Why is this place the last location I have to go to before I get to Ganon's kingdom?"

"Ah, yes, that is an excellent question. Your mother, Alice, knew you would be a little nervous, so she told me you will be here to rest for a bit. And you know, there is a lot of differences between an angel and a demon's personality," he stressed.

"Yeah, I barely ever see Mom looking stressed or anxious," I said, "compared to my dad, who I am sometimes afraid of," I confessed quietly to Alatar.

"That is normal because I too am scared of him sometimes myself."

"You do? Does everyone?" I asked.

"I suppose. Sometimes if he looks your way, you would think he was mad at you but that is just his normal facial expression."

Just then a little yellow fairy the size of a baseball poked out from another room and flew toward Alatar. She was a beautiful fairy and her wings sparkled. When she noticed me, she smiled and looked like she was batting her head toward me. She asked Alatar had she seen me before. He nodded and told her yes.

"Oh, Wolverine, you might not remember Holly, but she saw you when you were a baby as well. She would come with me to see you sometimes."

"Oh?" I said.

"Yes, every time you saw us, you were most excited about seeing Holly. She loved you so much and she would always make you laugh. But of course, you probably don't remember such things. You were really young."

Holly was nodding eagerly. I noticed something about her. She looked like she couldn't talk. It reminded me back on Earth of a well-known children's book, *Peter Pan*. There was a fairy in the story named Tinkerbell. Well, it's a story Madeline and Victoria told me about. Holly reminded me of Tinkerbell because Tinkerbell couldn't talk either.

When Holly noticed Niko sitting beside me, she went over and petted his head. Niko looked like he was enjoying it because his horns were moving. I told her his name was Niko. When she was done petting him, she went back to rest on Alatar's shoulder.

"Wolverine," Alatar began, "I am immensely proud of you. Especially because you have chosen to do what's best for your family. Even though you have decided not to kill Ganon, I think that will be the biggest achievement for you. I grant you great blessings on your way that his heart will change. Just be mindful that it might take some time."

"I know," I confessed. "I already knew that this was going to be harder than I thought it would be."

Alatar nodded and then told me I could wait here as long as I needed before I headed to Ganon's kingdom. I was grateful for the offer, but I was ready to get it over with. He understood.

As Niko and I moved toward the door, Alatar and Holly waved goodbye and I waved back at them.

I knew it was time. It was time to face my ultimate nemesis.

Ganon.

Chapter 13

Ganon's Kingdom

We were above the clouds again and it felt like there were thousands of butterflies in my stomach. My heart was beating rapidly, and I could feel my adrenaline increasing. But I tried to be calm as possible.

"Last destination, Ganon's kingdom. Nervous?" Niko asked me.

"I don't even know anymore. So many things have happened," I replied.

"You can do this, Wolverine. I know you can. Just don't think about what might happen. Focus on what you really need to focus on. Do you think you can do that?"

"Niko, you know that my response is usually, I'll try, but this time I'll say, OK."

"That's the spirit! Now let's get this over with like you said," Niko encouraged.

One hour passed before we saw the kingdom up ahead. That made my stomach hurt even worse. "We're here at last. Ready, Wolverine?" Niko asked again.

"I don't think so. My stomach's churning," I admitted.

"Wolverine, we can do this! I'm telling you," Niko pushed.

"OK, OK. You're right, I should be better than this. I think I might have a plan. Let's not land near the kingdom. Maybe a little further away so we're hidden." I suggested.

"Great idea! Let's land behind this big bush."

As we flew down behind the bush, we were silent so we wouldn't alarm the guards. "Great," I said. "Of course, there would be guards here. Now what are we going to do? Trick the guards somehow?"

"Don't worry. We'll use another tactic. Let's go sneak around the back. I bet there's another way in for sure. C'mon," Niko said. We sneakily ran to one bush at a time until we had finally made it to the back. "Good! A door."

"Is it locked?" I asked.

"I don't know," he said. As he tried to open the door it stayed shut.

"Let me try," I offered. When I tried to open it, it did the same thing with me as with Niko. "Yep. It's definitely not going to budge. We have to find another way."

"I'll try banging it down," Niko suggested.

"Are you crazy? They're gonna hear us! Let's just try the front entrance where the guards are," I suggested instead.

"No, we can't! That's a bad idea. We need to act in a smarter way. The front entrance isn't the best idea," Niko disagreed.

"Can't we trick 'em?"

"We can't. They're smarter than you think. Plus, they already know that you were coming," he reminded me.

"But banging down the door is going to make a racket!" I tried to get Niko to see reason.

"Trust me," Niko pleaded. "Let me just do it. Once we get through, we'll hide."

"OK," I agreed in annoyance.

As Niko tried to bust through the door, after the third strike the door crashed in, and we both quickly hid. We heard the guard's pounding, angry footsteps instantly searching for the source of the noise. As they left out through the door, we came out from our hiding spots and then we both exhaled in relief. "I kind of feel ashamed that your idea was much better than mine. Especially coming from a dragon," I whispered.

"You should be. Follow my lead," said Niko and laughed.

As Niko guided me, he led me to a door to open it. "OK, open the door. And be *very* quiet. You'll see why."

"OK," I nodded. When I opened the door, thousands of demons were all in this one giant room. It surprised me a little. "Oh, OK. Now I see," I said whispering again.

"Yeah, c'mon. We need to quietly go through this hallway because I want to free my friends who are locked in the room where I was once locked too. And I was thinking maybe one of them could help us," he told me.

"I will. Don't worry. I promise I won't make a peep—"

"Hello, Wolverine."

"Ahhh!" I shouted.

"Wolverine, are you serious! Now we're doomed because of you!" Niko said.

"Got you," a familiar voice hissed.

I looked back to see who scared me. It was that snake, Synthus! "You!" I was seething.

"I knew that I was going to get you. You did a fantastic job of alarming the demons. Now both of you are spotted!"

At that moment, all the demons turned our way with a surprised look on their faces. "Get them!" One of them ordered.

"Niko, we have to hide!" I told him.

"Down that hallway I was talking to you about! I'll tell you which room the dragons are in!" Niko instructed. We ran through the long hallway and entered through a door on the left. We shut the door quickly and heard the demons pass by. We then began to feel relieved. "Phew!" Niko said tiredly.

"Sorry," I apologized.

"It's fine. We're in the room where we need to be anyway. But we can't be in here for long," he warned.

"Right," I said.

As we looked in front of us, we saw cages dangling from the ceiling. It was a massive room with nothing but cages. When I looked at Niko, his face did not move an inch. All he was doing was glaring at them. He didn't look OK, so I asked after him. "Niko, are you alright?"

"This place," Niko started to say, "brings back such memories. Being locked in here with the rest."

I looked back at the cages again and started to realize this was the place where he was locked up with the other dragons. "Oh," I said with a sad realization.

He then shook his head and said, "Come on, we need to find my friend. He has to help us! His name is Dexter. We need to find out which cage he's in."

We both started to walk around while calling his name to see if he would answer. Our voices echoed and bounced along the walls. But we never heard a peep from any of the cages. As soon as we were about to give up, we heard a voice from a cage not too far from us. "Niko?"

"Dexter!" Niko yelled. He ran so fast toward the cage that Dexter was in that I couldn't keep up with him.

"Niko slow down!" I begged him.

Once we got to the cage, Niko quickly tried to free Dexter. Dexter was bewildered. "Niko, what are you doing?"

"I'm freeing you to help us stop Ganon!" Niko replied, still trying to help him get out.

"Us? Who's us?" Dexter asked Niko. As his eyes turned to me. "Niko, who is she?"

"Her name is Wolverine. She is the daughter of Alice and Amorok. The one Ganon always keeps bringing up. We are both here to stop Ganon."

"But how did you both even meet?" Dexter asked him.

"It doesn't matter right now," Niko said, ignoring the question. "Right now, we're just going to get you out of here so you can help us."

"I, I can't. I can't risk it. This is just all too much, Niko. Before, you were not like this. You were never so brave, and I've always told you to be strong but look at you now. You're wanting to defeat Ganon. How?"

"Wolverine encouraged me to be brave," Niko replied. "Dexter, you can help us and I know you can be brave too. Just trust me, alright?"

Dexter sighed as he shook his head side to side and responded, "No, Niko, I just can't. I know in the past I told you to be strong but, like I've said it's just too much. I'm sorry, but no. I can't do this."

I went in front of Niko and said to Dexter, "Why? Why are you afraid to take action to do what's right? If you help us, we will win and Ganon will stop doing what he's doing. We can even help the other dragons here that are wrongly locked in cages just like you. You may not know fully who I am, but I know the truth of why Ganon is doing this, and I can tell you this now, it is not because he can but it's because of his brother, Gydon. I don't have time to explain it all right now because the demons are looking for us. Please Dexter, help us turn his ways around."

"But why can't we kill him? If we kill him, he will not return to his habitual ways," Dexter explained.

"I promised Ganon's brother that I wouldn't. He will not turn back because he will remember what it was like being evil. He will know he will lose again. Now, for the last time … will you help us?" I pleaded.

Dexter looked at the both of us for a long moment and then replied, "OK. I'll try. Just get me out of this cage."

"I knew I could count on you, Dexter!" Niko said happily.

When we were almost done getting him out of the cage, the door that we came through quickly opened. In the next moment, we finally unlocked Dexter's cage. Dexter quickly jumped out and we all ran through the halls. When we went to open the doors, we didn't know it led to the big room where Ganon was.

We opened the door and there he was. Ganon's eyes and the veins in his arms were a bright orange.

"Where do you think you're going?" Ganon asked calmly with his arms folded.

The area behind him looked like the area I was in when I was talking to Ganon in my dream. And it was! I could see Niko and Dexter trembling in their fear as Ganon glared at us. I was also trembling, but I decided to speak up.

"Niko, Dexter, and I all changed our minds about killing you."

Ganon was stunned. "What? So why are you here if you're not going to defeat me?"

"We're here to stop you from being immoral and Dexter decided to help us," I told him.

"*All of us are going to make you to stop being immoral and Dexter decided to help us,*" Ganon mocked. "Tch, who came up with that foolish idea?"

I immediately replied, "Your brother did."

His face quickly turned into a frown, and he stuttered, "G-Gydon asked you not to kill me?'

"Yes," I answered.

He then looked at me in disbelief. "Why? Why does he not want me killed after all the hurtful things I've said and done?"

"Because he still loves you, Ganon, and that's what love is about. He told me to tell this to you and he begged me to find a way to change you. He told me he visited you one

160

day and when he saw you kill Atlas, he said he immediately left because he felt you would never change."

"What?" His eyes widened.

"I asked him was he ever going to see you again and he responded, no."

At that moment Ganon looked miserable and asked, "Is there any way I could go see him?"

"Ganon, you need to accept the responsibility for the things that you have done first. You have to change for yourself first before going to your brother and asking for forgiveness. I have a question for you. I asked Gydon today why you hated him in the first place, and he implied that he didn't know. Why do you hate Gydon?" I pushed.

Ganon sighed deeply with his right hand on his forehead. Then he answered quietly. "I never wanted a brother."

"What?" I said as I scrunched my face.

"I SAID, I NEVER WANTED A BROTHER!" He screamed at me.

I jumped. Even Dexter and Niko jumped, quite surprised.

"That's ... why?" I asked.

"YES! Couldn't you have figured that out before coming here?" Then he sighed and said, "I'm sorry I yelled."

"More like screaming to me," boasted Niko.

Everyone, including me stared at Niko.

That's when Ganon lost it again. "You know what? All of you leave! I'm done! Just go back to where you came from!"

"But, boss, what are we going to do with the rest of the stuff we had to defeat Wolverine?" Agwel, asked coming out of nowhere.

"Just cancel it all. I don't want to do this anymore. This was a waste of time because my plan happened for nothing," he told them.

The rest of the demons looked at each other nervously and were not sure if they should. So, they just stood there in shock.

"Are all of you deaf?! CANCEL IT!"

The demons quickly began cancelling everything they'd worked hard preparing to use to destroy me. Meanwhile, Ganon shoved us out the main doors of his kingdom as he left too.

"Where are you going?" I shouted towards him.

"None of your business," he responded rudely. The doors of the kingdom slammed shut, causing Niko, Dexter, and me to jump.

I sighed gruffly and admonished Niko, "Really, Niko? You had to tell him that? That was ridiculous!"

"Niko, what were you thinking?" Dexter asked, also frustrated.

"Sorry, OK?" Niko apologized.

"Whatever. It's fine," I said after some time. "But what are we going to do now? We don't even know where Ganon's going."

I noticed Agwel glaring at me, so I glared back at him.

"Who knows," responded Dexter. "But I think we should go back inside and free the dragons from their cages."

"Good idea," Niko agreed.

Because Ganon had canceled the attack against me, the guards had no problem letting us back in and the demons were too busy canceling all the things they had planned to notice us. As we went inside the room with the dangling cages again, we noticed that most of the dragons were asleep. So, we called to the ones who weren't.

"Hello, can anybody hear me?" Dexter asked.

"Dexter?" A voice answered.

As we turned our heads around to the female voice that called Dexter's name, Dexter said, "Jasper?" He ran quickly toward the cage that we had heard it from. When we were at Jasper's cage, I noticed she looked very beautiful. She had gorgeous sparkly scales and big wings. The color of her scales and her wings were a midnight lavender, and her eyes were that same color.

"Jasper, I'm going to free you and all of the dragons here," Dexter said.

"What? No! You can't! We're going to be in big trouble with Ganon!" she protested.

"No, you won't! Ganon canceled everything and he left!" Dexter told her.

"Huh?" Jasper questioned. "So that means he's not going to be evil anymore?"

"We are not sure about that," Dexter confessed. "We don't even know where he ran off to."

"All … three?" she asked.

"This is Wolverine. She is from The Two Kingdoms," Niko offered.

"The daughter of Alice and Amorok?" Jasper questioned further.

"Yeah, how did you know?" Niko asked.

"My mother often told me the story of her and her family when I was little. During the time Wolverine was a baby."

"Oh. Anyway, we really need to get you out of this cage so you can help us free more of the dragons," Dexter explained.

"Alrighty," Jasper said. "Get me out of this cramped cage."

As we unlocked Jasper's cage, she promptly went to free more of the dragons. That helped us out a whole bunch. The last dragon we had to free was the hardest one. It was a female, and I didn't think she would ever budge. Her name was Fizzlespit, which was a very unusual name.

"Fizzlespit, come on! We need to free you!" Niko pleaded.

"I won't come out, you cold corndog! It will never happen!" She snarled.

After a lot of begging, she finally came out. Phew! Then, as we went outside, all of them said their goodbyes and leaped toward the sky to go home where they really belonged.

"Well, I think I should join them," Dexter said. "Goodbye to the both of you."

When Dexter was about to leave, Niko stopped him and asked, "Wait. You're leaving already?"

"Of course," replied Dexter. "I need to go back home. But Niko, aren't you coming too?"

Niko looked at me then back at Dexter and responded, "I will go back home when we sort out Ganon. So maybe soon."

Dexter nodded and said, "OK, goodbye! I can't wait to see you again so you can tell me how you stopped him." We watched him fly into the air to catch up with the other dragons.

Niko turned to me and asked, "Well, where should we go from here?"

"Maybe we should go back to Orker Village," I suggested. "It's kind of getting late anyway."

"OK," agreed Niko.

As we arrived back at Orker Village, I quickly got off Niko's back and hurried toward Leon who was just coming out of a shop.

"Leon!" I shouted.

Leon was confused which direction the voice was coming from, but he did recognize my voice. "Wolverine? Why have you come back? Weren't you supposed to defeat Ganon?"

"About that," I started as Niko caught up with me, "before I even knew about this, I met Gydon, and he begged me not to kill Ganon. So, I promised him. When I told Ganon that Gydon didn't want me to kill him, he started asking to go see him, but I told him that he can't go back if he doesn't change. After Niko antagonized him because he was shouting at me, Ganon told his demons to cancel everything and then he left. We're just here because we were not sure where to go or what to do next. Do you think we could stay here for the night?"

"Of course," Leon nodded.

"Thanks. Also, do you have any idea where Ganon might have run off to?"

"I'm not entirely sure but If I could guess maybe to Gydon, perhaps?" Leon suggested.

My eyes grew wide in agreement. "That's right. Actually, I changed my mind. Come on, Niko, we're going back to Gydon's kingdom," I said with excitement.

"What? But why, Wolverine? Plus, I'm so tired!"

"We won't be there for long," I told Niko. "I just want to see what he's going to do."

"I can't believe this," Niko groaned.

"Be quiet and come on!" I strictly ordered him.

When we arrived at Gydon's kingdom, I realized Thallus and the other guard were not there. The sun was setting to night over the horizon now. As I went to see if the kingdom doors were locked, I discovered that surprisingly, they weren't. I opened the doors. There was no one out and about so Niko and I were able to sneak inside the kingdom.

"OK, why are we here again?" Niko questioned.

"To figure out why Ganon is here, if he's here," I explained.

"Oh, right," Niko replied.

As we walked alongside the hallways, I heard faint voices. It sounded like they were coming from the library where I spoke with Gydon earlier. "Shhh! Niko, they're in the library," I whispered.

"Ganon, I can't forgive you if you're not sure if you want to quit or not. If I forgive you, I need to be sure you are not going to be evil again. I don't want to go through this conversation again," said Gydon.

"Gydon, please. Just give me one more chance. I've hurt you badly in the past and it was a terrible mistake. But I won't be the way I was ever again. Please trust me, Gydon," Ganon begged.

Gydon sighed and said, "How can I?"

"Trust me. I promise I will change," Ganon replied.

"Just give me time to think," Gydon said as he looked down at the ground.

The room was silent for a minute or two and then Ganon said, "You can't even look at me, can you?"

"Ganon, no it's just that … that this all too stressful to me. Talking to you like this was what I wanted way back. Having a one-on-one conversation with you, it's just really difficult. Please, just give me some time to think. Maybe I will be able to change my mind afterward."

Ganon shook his head and responded, "No, you won't," then headed toward the door.

"Oh shoot," I whispered. I quickly moved out of the way as the door clicked open.

When Ganon opened the door and saw me and Niko he said, "Oh. Well, surprise, surprise. I can't believe you were listening to me pleading to that fool. Just get out of my way. Everything is just a waste for me now."

As he walked away, I shouted, "That's not true! There's still hope!"

"Let him go, Wolverine. I know I told him to be persistent, but he will never let it go."

I looked back at Gydon with a sad expression on my face and said, "No. I have to help him. There's still hope, but it just hasn't touched him quite yet." Niko and I ran for Ganon.

"Ganon, Ganon please! Just let him think. Why are you doing this!"

"Leave me alone!" He scowled. "Why do you care?"

"Because this conflict is not good for you or your brother. I have a friend on Earth who works at a Chinese restaurant named Li Jun and he's having problems with his brother as well. You're not alone! Brothers have conflict."

Ganon quickly covered his eyes with one of his hands and made a silent sigh. This got me worried. "Ganon, are you alright?" No words came out. Not even a sound. Niko and I looked at each other, then back at him.

"Wolverine … I'm sorry," he managed to whimper out. "Forgive me. I have done such horrible things. I have made everything worse for myself, and others. Especially Gydon. I promise I will never go back to what I was before. Please accept my apology?" He asked, staring down at the ground.

I could tell he was sobbing, and his words caused a tear to fall down my cheek. Even Niko had a tear running down his face. After a long moment of silence I said, "Yes."

Ganon looked at me and his eyes looked redder than normal. "Do you think you could make Gydon forgive me?"

"I don't have the power to make him, but I could try to encourage him," I promised. "Let's go, Niko."

When I went to Gydon I told him, "Gydon, please forgive your brother. He's telling you the truth and he really wants to change. He even apologized to me. He doesn't want to be evil anymore. Please give him a chance. He is devastated."

"I've made up my mind, Wolverine," Gydon told me. "I will accept my brother's apology."

"Really?" I smiled, knowing I'd fulfilled and accomplished something far greater than I could ever imagine. "Thank you. He promised he would never go back to the way he was before."

"I just hope he won't," Gydon said cautiously.

I nodded and ran back to Ganon who was still standing in the same spot, against the wall, looking at the ground. "He forgives you," I told him.

That caught Ganon off guard. "He, he does?"

"Yes," I responded.

Ganon looked the other way and said, "Thank you, Wolverine."

"You're welcome," I said back.

A vibration on my right wrist was beeping and realized it was my tracker. I noticed the percentage bar showed a hundred percent and the tracker was beeping.

"I think Niko and I should be going right now."

Niko and I hurried toward the main doors of Gydon's kingdom. We decided to spend the night at Orker Village.

So, we rode off into the night sky to sleep and rest, there.

Chapter 14

"Hello Again!"

The morning sun was bright while the birds chirped songs and people went busily to their destinations. I woke up early. The time beside me indicated it was a quarter past nine. I heard a sound and a vibration on my wrist. The tracker showed the percentage bar again but this time below it there was a button displayed and the words: "Complete."

That must mean it is time to go back to The Two Kingdoms. I need to go tell Niko about this!

Before I went to Niko, I decided to go eat breakfast first. When I finished, I found Niko and told him about the thing that was on my tracker. Niko was already awake when I got to where he was.

"Niko, you won't believe this. We're done!" I said thrilled.

"With the mission?" He yawned.

"Yes! Now we can finally go back! Aren't you excited, Niko?" I questioned.

"What? Of course, I am!" He replied as he turned to my side.

"Then let's press it!" I said.

"Woah, woah, woah! Press what?" He asked me.

"This button on my tracker screen. It can teleport us back to The Two Kingdoms," I explained.

"Wait, first we have to say goodbye to Leon and thank him for letting us stay here for the night. We can't just leave like that," he explained back.

"You're right. Sorry, I was just too impatient. Let's go tell Leon that we're leaving."

We found him at a supermarket. "Leon, thank you for letting us stay the night again," I told him.

"You're welcome. You're leaving?" He asked.

"Yes," I replied. "We're done with everything so now we are returning to The Two Kingdoms. We're just here because we just wanted to say goodbye."

"Oh, well, goodbye. It was nice seeing you, Wolverine, and of course you too, Niko," he said.

"Goodbye," Niko and I both said.

Then, I looked at Niko and asked, "Are you ready?"

"Definitely!" Niko said.

I pressed the button on my tracker instantly Niko and I were teleported back to the outside of Aunt Cornelia's house with Aunt Cornelia and Alice right in front of us. They were both smiling but Aunt Cornelia's grin was the biggest. "We made it!" I was bursting full of joy.

"Yes, child, you have stopped Ganon. So, we will have a feast at The Two Kingdoms to celebrate your victory!" Aunt Cornelia said.

Niko and I smiled at each other, knowing we had worked hard even though we had difficulties.

"Come along now, we don't need to be late now, do we?" She asked.

"No, ma'am, Aunt Cornelia," I replied. Then all of us walked from Aunt Cornelia's house to The Angelic Kingdom. When we got inside, each and every angel and demon was busy setting up a long golden table with white fabric laid on it. "Wow!" I said, stunned.

"This is all for you and your bravery, Wolverine. You helped this kingdom with your faith, so we have all decided to celebrate you for it," she explained.

I sighed and said, "I just, never knew I would come this far."

"Wolverine!" Familiar voices called from behind.

When I turned around, I felt my heart skip a beat. "Madeline! Victoria!" I ran quickly into their arms, bawling tears.

"We've missed you!" Madeline said.

"I miss you both too!" I said back.

After we stopped hugging, Alice went up to the front to speak. As she was walking up, the demons and the angels were almost done setting things up. "Alright, girls go and pick a seat!" Aunt Cornelia told us. I noticed Amorok standing beside Alice at the front.

"OK," all three of us said in unison.

Victoria, Madeline, and I decided to sit in the three chairs that were right in front of us. Niko went to stand next to a guard. When we were seated, I recognized Tydus walking by in front of our table, so I said, "Tydus!"

He turned toward me and smiled then kept walking. Madeline and Victoria were curious, so Victoria asked, "Who was that?"

"He's my brother," I answered her. "Tydus used to work for Ganon but he told me that he didn't want to work for him any longer. So, he quit."

"Oh. Also, I have another question. Who was that dragon that was with you earlier?"

I looked at Niko who was looking around beside the angel guard. Then I smiled and explained to her, "That's Niko. He helped me throughout my journey. He used to be a slave of Ganon's, though, he wasn't the only one. Multiple dragons were captured as Ganon's slaves. I met him when an angel named Gabriel brought him here when Ganon kicked him out. Gabriel asked if anyone could keep him. I told Gabriel I could, but he didn't believe that I could take care of him, so he refused to let me keep him. Then Alice told him to let me have him, so he did. And that's how we fought and fought together." After I told them that I noticed Alatar and Holly were here. That made me even more cheerful.

"Hmph, I wish I had a dragon." Madeline said.

"Don't," I said. "They're a lot to handle. Especially when they're smarter than you."

We all laughed and patiently waited in silence for Alice to speak. While we were waiting, all the angels and the demons started to sit down until none were left standing. Except for the guards. Then Alice spoke. "Thank you all for being here and thank you, Wolverine, for destroying Ganon for the sake of our kingdom. Me, Amorok, and everyone else is deeply honored. Is there anything you would like to say to our royal family?"

My heart raced because I didn't know if I should tell everyone that I didn't kill Ganon. I looked over at Alatar and Holly and he nodded at me knowing that something was going to happen after I confessed. I knew I couldn't lie to them, and I needed them to know the truth. So, I slowly replied, "I … I didn't defeat Ganon."

Everyone was shocked at my answer. Even Tydus, Victoria and Madeline were as well. But the only people who weren't shocked an inch were Aunt Cornelia, Alatar, and Holly.

"Wolverine, you didn't kill Ganon?" Amorok said as he came up in front of Alice.

Before I could speak, Aunt Cornelia replied, "No. In fact, she did exactly what she was supposed to. Yes, she didn't kill Ganon but she had courage to change him and—"

Amorok couldn't bear it anymore, so he made a noise so loud like an evil dragon to stop Aunt Cornelia from speaking. That shocked everyone, including Alice. Holly hid behind Alatar, peeking behind his shoulder. I had never in my life heard a demon yell. I guess when demons get angry and yell, they sound like an angry dragon coming to eat you alive. It was so loud it rang in my ears.

"Amorok, please calm down. You're scaring everyone here. Just listen to what she has to say. Maybe she can explain to all of us why Wolverine hasn't killed Ganon," Alice told him.

He grunted and said, "Fine. Explain."

His eyes were so scary that it frightened me to even look at him.

"Your Highness, Wolverine did not kill him because she found out Ganon's brother, Gydon, did not want him to be killed. You know how your daughter is. She wants to discover the *best* ways to fix problems and instead of killing Ganon she had to change him and—"

Then Amorok yelled again. "That doesn't mean anything, old woman! Just because she changed Ganon doesn't mean he's never going back to being evil! Wolverine, explain yourself!"

"Amorok! Why can't you just listen to what my mother has to say?! You're being ignorant! Calm down!" Alice shouted at Amorok.

"Understanding someone's problem is better than just killing them," I boasted out as I stood up.

Everyone stared at me, even the guards. Amorok stopped yelling at Alice and immediately turned to me. Then I spoke again. "If you don't *listen* to what their problem is, then you won't understand it because you have never walked in their shoes. Why is it so hard for you to listen?"

There, I explained myself. I thought.

I sat back down slowly because I didn't think I was supposed to talk to him like that.

Everyone's eyes were on Amorok now. He was so mad that he scoffed and walked away, murmuring. The room was steady and quiet now until Alice began to say, "Sorry about this everyone, please enjoy the feast, thank you." Then to Amorok, she said, "Amorok! We can talk about this later!"

After that everything kind of went back to normal. My friends didn't say anything to me because they didn't want to stress me out.

Did I hear my mother say that Aunt Cornelia was her mother?

While we ate, I told my friends more about my journey.

Then I heard Alice call to me to the room where Amorok was. Even though I knew he was probably going to apologize for what he did earlier, it still made me a little nervous. I followed Alice inside the room where Amorok was. He instantly got up and apologized. I received his apology, but I still thought about the way he yelled at Aunt Cornelia. It had frightened me deeply.

I returned to the feast and saw Ariella and Leroy with Aunt Cornelia, Madeline, and Victoria. When I walked up to them, Aunt Cornelia noticed me, so she told Leroy and Ariella to send them back to Earth. "Goodbye, Wolverine!" Victoria and Madeline hugged.

"Goodbye!" I hugged back.

When they left, I asked Aunt Cornelia if they'd come back to visit me one day and she said yes. I was thrilled. Then she started to say something else. "Wolverine, please come with me. I have something very important to share if you don't mind?"

"Not at all, Aunt Cornelia," I said.

"Great. We will be going back to my house." When we arrived back at her home, she said, "I know you probably are wondering why I wanted you here, but I know you've had questions along your journey that have not been answered. Questions about the orbs, the silver crystal, Aveline, and Synthus. Haven't you?"

"I've had questions about the orbs and the crystal, but I haven't had any concerns about Aveline and Synthus," I admitted.

"OK well, before I answer those concerns, I will tell you this. Child, I am your grandmother," she confessed.

My eyes lit up. "So, I did hear Alice refer to you as her mother during the feast!"

"Yes, child. Now, I will answer all four of your questions. Number one, the orbs. The fairies made these orbs just for you. That box under your bed and the letter in it was written by me," she explained. "But since you didn't get to read it, I will read it to you now."

"OK," I nodded.

She picked up the piece of paper that was in the box and read:

> *Dear Wolverine,*
>
> *Here is this special orb that you will use for your journey. It allows you to be able to talk to animals, so it ought to make your journey a little bit easier. My helpers, the fairies, have made this orb. I hope you will put this to good use because this was a gift. Good luck on your journey and stay blessed.*
>
> *Your beloved grandmother,*
> *Aunt Cornelia*

When she was done reading the letter I said, "Wow, just for me?"

"Just for you," she repeated. "I knew you would have to travel a long distance and I knew you would encounter Atlas, that old tiger. He used to be so different when he was alive. Now he's nothing but mean and cares only about himself."

"I can see that," I agreed.

"Number two," Aunt Cornelia continued, "the silver crystal. Agwel told Ganon that you had it, but actually I had it all along. Agwel lied to Ganon because he wanted you to worry and to feel insecure. He wanted you to get off track. This gem," she said as she picked it up, "is for doing powerful magic. Only wizards like me who have a lot of experience in magic can handle it. Ganon never had a lot of experience with magic so he couldn't have it. He wanted it badly for his plan to stop you, so he told his demons to go out and look for it."

"I see," I said.

"Number three is about Aveline. She used to live on Earth in London with her parents and her older brother until one day when she went to sleep her dreams suddenly captured her inside so she couldn't leave. She's been living in that scary-looking mansion ever since with that dragon. Poor child."

"Man, I feel bad. So basically, she's dreaming but it's like she's trapped and can't get out of it. Is there a way to free her?" I asked.

"There is. But the ingredients are so far away. Farther than Ganon's kingdom. I have only one of them and that is this silver crystal. I do wish I could help in some sort of way. They're just too far," she explained sadly.

I looked down at the ground with a sigh.

"Don't worry about it too much, Wolverine. I know one day we will be able to," she winked at me.

"Alright," I said.

"Now the last one, Synthus. His story of how he started working for Ganon is pretty sad. Before he worked for him, he was a lonely snake who could barely provide for himself. One day, Ganon saw him, and he decided to make Synthus work for him. He made him drink a potion that would make him forget his past and would make him wicked."

"Yeah, that is pretty sad," I agreed. "Aunt Cornelia, how did you know all of these events happened?"

She nodded and replied, "You'll see one day. Anyway, you may go, child. There's nothing else I have to say to you any longer."

"OK. Thank you, Aunt Cornelia, for this conversation. I will be going now," I told her.

"Safe travels."

As I was walked back toward The Two Kingdoms, I realized Atlas was on the right side of me, smiling. I smiled back at him and then he disappeared into nothingness.

Then, I heard a little squeaky voice from a bush, so I went to see who was making that sound. As I crouched down beside the thick bush, out popped out a bunny. It looked a little familiar. It was the same bunny from when I was in training. He remembered me! I picked him up and told him, "It looks like you're coming with me, little guy. I hope my parents won't mind that you're going to stay with me. And you know what? I'll call you Widget! C'mon, let's go!"

Then I walked Widget and myself back all the way to The Angelic Kingdom.

About the Author

Writing Journey

Award Winning Author Kelsey Thomas is a youth author who lives in Central Arkansas. Her debut novel, "Call of The Wolves" is an exciting fantasy fiction novel written when she was eleven years old.

Now at thirteen, her new book, "The Two Kingdoms" is another great read for those who love fiction.

Kelsey enjoys playing with her three-year-old havachon, Pepper who is a handful but worth it!

Kelsey has always enjoyed writing and telling stories as a young child. Perhaps it was inevitable that she would call grappling with words and language a career—and loving every moment. She is privileged to share her work with a large and welcoming audience.

Get in touch to discover more about her work, writing process and future endeavors.

"We Make Good Great."

www.butterflytypeface.com

www.ingramcontent.com/pod-product-compliance
Lightning Source LLC
Chambersburg PA
CBHW051124260626
47170CB00005B/1647

9 781951 883478